First American Edition 2015
Kane Miller, A Division of EDC Publishing

Text Copyright © 2014 Kate Welshman
Illustration and Design Copyright © Hardie Grant Egmont 2014
First published in Australia by Hardie Grant Egmont 2014

For information contact:
Kane Miller, A Division of EDC Publishing
P.O. Box 470663
Tulsa, OK 74147-0663
www.kanemiller.com
www.edcpub.com
www.usbornebooksandmore.com

Library of Congress Control Number: 2014950300

Printed and bound in the United States of America
5 6 7 8 9 10
ISBN: 978-1-61067-387-7

Choose *your* own Ever After

MAKE UP *or* Break Up

BY KATE WELSHMAN

Kane Miller
A DIVISION OF EDC PUBLISHING

Chapter One

"Ally's into hunks," I heard Mum say to our neighbor Mrs. Rickson. "She has a poster of Chris Hemsworth stuck to the ceiling of her bedroom."

Mum and Mrs. Rickson were having coffee in our kitchen, and the window was wide open. I was studying for a Latin test on the lawn in the backyard, right under the window. I could hear every word they were saying.

"They grow up so quickly these days, don't they?" Mrs. Rickson said.

"Ally's a bit of a late developer," said Mum. "But she's just as boy crazy as all her friends."

I rolled my eyes. *Late developer?* How embarrassing.

"Well," Mrs. Rickson said with a sigh, "my Tony's shy around girls these days."

Tony Rickson was in my year at school. He was a long-haired muso nerd.

"He's crazy about piano, though," she continued. "I never have to nag him to practice."

"It's a shame that Ally and Tony don't spend time together anymore," said Mum. "They used to be such good friends."

I felt my phone vibrating in my pocket. A message. Thank goodness. I wasn't sure I wanted to hear what Mum and Mrs. Rickson had to say about Tony and me. That was so ancient history.

I pulled out my phone and opened the message. It was from my best friend, Cat.

If you don't come and help me with Latin now, I'll have to cheat on the test tomorrow.

Chuckling, I closed my textbook and went inside.

"Mum, I'm going to Cat's place to study," I called from the kitchen doorway.

"Hello, Ally," said Mrs. Rickson.

"Hi, Mrs. Rickson." I stood clutching my Latin book to my chest so she couldn't tell that I really was a "late developer," like Mum had said.

I was sure they'd go into my room after I left to look at my poster of Chris Hemsworth. Then Mrs. Rickson would go home and tell Tony all about it. "*I don't know why Ally Motbey thinks a hunk like Chris Hemsworth would be interested in her,*" she'd say to Tony. "*She's totally flat-chested.*"

"All right, but be back for dinner," said Mum. "No later than six."

"Okay. Bye, Mum. Bye, Mrs. Rickson."

"No later than six!" I heard Mum shout as I raced to the front door.

"*Okay.* Geez …" I muttered, slamming the door behind me.

It was a short walk to Cat's house – just twelve minutes through the park. *It's funny,* I thought as I walked, *how I'm always late home from Cat's place even though it's so close by.* Something happened when we were together. It was like time flew or something. Like the planet started spinning faster, and in the blink of an eye two hours were gone. I guess that was why we were best friends. But it also meant I was always late for dinner!

Cat and I had been besties since the dawn of time. Well, since grade 5, when we had detention together after squeezing tubes of paint down the art room sink. Cat's full name was Caterina-Cordelia Fini. Her father, Carlo Fini, was a famous fashion designer and her mother, Gina, used to be a model. Their house was a white two story with a triple garage and a really long driveway. It was huge.

It's definitely the biggest house in the street, I thought as I walked up their driveway.

Cat's mum answered the front door, smiling. She always seemed happy to see me. "Cat's upstairs, studying," she said, motioning me inside. "She said you might drop in this afternoon."

"Hi, Gina," I said, kissing her first on one cheek and then the other. She and Cat were the only people I knew who were sophisticated enough to kiss both cheeks like that.

Gina wasn't like my mum or Mrs. Rickson. Gina wore rompers – not sweats – and her fingernails and toenails were always painted the same color. She and Cat looked more like sisters than mother and daughter. She wouldn't even let me call her "Mrs. Fini." She said it made her feel old.

I ran up the stairs to Cat's room. She was stretched out on her stomach, with headphones on, her toes tapping to the music. I looked around for her Latin book. It was on her desk. I sat on the end of her bed.

"Ally!" she squealed. She pulled off her headphones and crawled across the bed to sit next to me. We kissed on both cheeks.

"Studying hard, Cat?" I asked, innocently.

She threw her hands in the air and groaned. "It's been doing my head in! I just can't handle Latin verbs. I mean, I totally get why Latin's a dead language … those Romans must have died of boredom trying to learn it."

I laughed, and then looked at her questioningly. "I still don't get it," I said, shaking my head. "I mean, you're Italian. Latin should be a cinch for you."

"Yeah, but we never speak Italian at home," Cat said. Then she grinned. "Well, only the swearwords ... and I don't think Hawky will test us on those."

Hawky, or Mrs. Hawkins, was our Latin teacher. Even though she was strict and most of the other kids thought she was an ogre, she was my favorite teacher, and Latin was my favorite subject.

A couple of years ago, our school introduced Latin classes starting from grade 7. Not everyone was thrilled. To say Latin wasn't Cat's favorite subject would be the understatement of the millennium. She relied on me to help her study.

I knew Cat would avoid studying for as long as she could, so I grabbed the Latin textbook from her desk. I turned to the verb table in the fourth chapter. For tomorrow's test we had to memorize the Latin verb *amare* – "to love."

"*Amo?*" I asked, looking at Cat. It meant "I love." Even Cat knew that much.

Cat flopped back onto the bed and closed her eyes, screwing up her face as if in tremendous pain.

"Come on," I said. "*Amo*. What does it mean?" I raised my eyebrows, waiting for an answer.

"A mo," replied Cat, a grin erupting on her face, "would be a bad look on you. Uh-uh, Ally. I don't think a moustache would suit you at all. I'd seriously have to reconsider my position as your bestie if you grew a mo."

I slammed the textbook shut and fixed her with a serious look. "Cat! You're going to flunk this test if you don't make an effort. Do you want me to help you or not?"

"*Amo*," said Cat slowly, "means 'I love' – as in *amo* Ollie."

I rolled my eyes. Ollie Haas, a grade 10 boy, was *the* hottest guy at our school. He was perfect. Tall, blond and athletic, Ollie was good at almost everything, especially music and drama.

Cat loved singing and drama, too, and had performed with Ollie in the school musical last year. All the girls in the musical – including Cat – had been falling over themselves to get close to him. In the end he'd ended up with the female lead – a girl in the year above him! – at the after party. The hottest news around the lockers was that they'd broken up over the summer and Ollie was back on the market.

Since she'd found out, Cat had hardly been able to talk about anything else. And then last week, when she found out that this year's school musical was about to be announced, she'd gone into overdrive. She'd been talking about Ollie almost nonstop for a full week now – saying how she was going to star opposite him in the musical in a lead role, and how he would fall in love with her.

It didn't really surprise me that she couldn't focus on Latin. Her head was totally filled up with dreams of stardom and her Ollie romance! But as her best friend I decided it was my duty to keep her from failing Latin, so I cast my eyes back to the verb table.

"*Amas*," I said.

Cat pouted and narrowed her green eyes. "Don't know."

"Yes, you do. Come on."

"It means, 'you love.' I know that. But who? Who do *you* love, Ally?"

I didn't hesitate. "I love Chris Hemsworth."

"*Pfft!* Doesn't count. He's famous … *and* he's married now."

"I know. But when it's just the two of us, alone in my room –" I started.

"Ally!" Cat scolded. "You need a *real* guy. I mean, I'll be going out with Ollie soon and you'll need a boyfriend, too." A thoughtful look crossed her face. "Actually, you know who's been looking pretty hot lately?"

"Who?"

"Your neighbor. The pianist."

For some reason, whenever someone said the word "pianist" it sent me completely silly. It was just one of those words, like "spatchcock." I started to giggle. "You mean Tony Rickson?"

"Yeah. Are you laughing because it's true or because I said 'pianist'?"

"Because you said 'pianist,'" I said firmly. "C'mon, Cat. Tony looks like a grunge rocker from the nineties."

"Trust me, under all that hair lies a total hottie," said Cat, stretching her arms behind her head. She considered herself an authority on who really was and wasn't a hottie underneath it all. "He's a diamond in the rough."

"More like an ugly hunk of quartz," I muttered. I studied the verb table intently.

"So, you admit he's a hunk."

"I'm not admitting anything," I said, starting to feel annoyed. "I wouldn't go near him, Cat."

"But he used to hang around you like a bad smell – and you used to let him," Cat said. "Remember?"

It felt like an accusation. Of course I remembered. For a short time last year, Tony and I had almost been more than just friends. But then something had happened – something I'd never told Cat about. I could feel my cheeks getting warm. I turned away, hoping Cat wouldn't notice.

"C'mon, Ally," she said, sitting up straight. "We're fourteen now. You totally need a boyfriend. And besides, I'll need you and Tony to come on double dates with me and Ollie."

I didn't say anything.

"You're blushing," said Cat with a giggle. "And your face looked far, *far* away."

I lifted the textbook, holding it up to my face. "*Amat*." I said sternly. "What does it mean?" I peered over the book at Cat.

She was still smiling smugly. "Are you wearing a bra?" she asked.

I put the book down and crossed my arms over my chest. "I don't wear one all the time," I said. "I don't need to. Not like you."

Cat looked down at her cleavage and clicked her tongue. "Yeah, but you've got *something*."

"What does any of this have to do with Latin?" I asked.

"What exactly does Latin have to do with anything?" she countered, flopping back onto the bed.

Exasperated, I threw myself down beside her. We looked at each other and giggled. Cat reached for her phone and took a photo of us.

I checked out the picture. My eyes were half closed and Cat was grinning like a maniac. The end of my blond braid looked like it was slithering into her ear. We both cracked up, then Cat deleted the photo.

"C'mon, let's get some gelato," she said. "Dad made a huge batch of hazelnut last night."

I wasn't sure what hazelnut gelato had to do with bras or Latin or Tony Rickson, but it did sound like a good idea. We crept down the stairs to the kitchen, tiptoeing past Cat's parents, who were both reading in the family room.

Mr. Fini burst into the kitchen as Cat opened the freezer door. He rolled up the newspaper he'd been reading and pretended to beat Cat's legs with it. "Caterina! This is the last bowl before dinner!"

"Okay, Dad," giggled Cat, slapping away the rolled up paper.

Mr. Fini grinned at me. He was short and round, and looked more like an Italian chef than a fashion designer. "Good afternoon, Ally. How are you?" He always spoke formally, with a faint Italian accent.

"Fine, thank you. Your gelato looks so delicious," I answered, watching Cat scoop it into bowls.

"It's my new gelato machine. It turns out perfectly every time!" Mr. Fini slapped a kiss on Cat's forehead and went back to the other room.

"Your dad's so fun," I said.

"He seems fun," said Cat, with a snort. "But you know how strict he is."

I nodded, but Mr. Fini didn't seem all that strict to me. Cat got away with almost everything. She just hated it when anyone – including her parents – got in the way of her plans. But I didn't say that. I just threw another spoonful of gelato down the hatch … and another … and another …

We ended up eating two huge bowls each. Then Cat put on Mr. Fini's Andrea Bocelli CD. We tried to sing along to the *Time to Say Goodbye* duet, but our throats were so cold and phlegmy from eating so much gelato, we sounded like Kermit the Frog. When our duet was over, we heard Mr. Fini giving us a slow clap from the next room. He'd heard the whole thing! We laughed until our faces were hot and tears were rolling down our cheeks.

Then it was time for Cat to walk me home. The suburb where we lived, Cherrywood, was just outside the city. It was green and leafy, with big houses and perfect gardens. Even though the trip across the park was twelve minutes door to door, it often took us more than an hour to walk each other home. Cat would walk me home, but then we'd still have more to say, so I'd walk her back home. Then when we got back to her place, the conversation would still be flowing, so she'd have to walk me home, and so on. We'd continue like this until it got dark or our parents yelled at us to come inside. Cat and I never ran out of things to talk about – not once.

This afternoon was no different – we walked back and forth, talking and laughing. I even got Cat singing Latin verbs. I couldn't believe I hadn't thought of it earlier. Cat could learn anything if she got to sing it.

At the end of the fifth trip around, Dad was standing in our driveway with his arms folded. "That's enough, girls," he said. He knew exactly what we were up to.

"But Mr. Motbey," pleaded Cat. "Ally always walks *me* to *my* place last."

Dad pretended to play a violin, his face contorted with mock grief. I giggled.

Cat pouted. "I just don't feel safe walking on my own," she said, shivering for effect. "And it's getting dark."

Dad reached into his pocket and jangled his car keys. "I can drive you home," he offered.

Cat gave me a withering glare, and I shot her a "What can I do?" look in reply.

"Don't worry," she told my dad grumpily. "I'll just walk by myself."

"*Amo* you, Caterina-Cordelia Fini," I said.

"*Amo* you too, Alexandra Motbey," said Cat with a little smile.

We hugged, and kissed each other on both cheeks.

"What a drama queen," said Dad after she left.

"She is *not*!" I said crossly. I stormed off, with Cat-like huffiness, into the house. I didn't want to hear anyone say anything against Cat. Even though, secretly, I kind of knew Dad was right.

I lay on my bed and looked up at Chris Hemsworth.

"That's the thing about Cat," I told him in a secretive voice. "She blows everything out of proportion. If I tell her the truth about Tony ..." But I couldn't finish the sentence, not even to Chris, and he was the best listener in the world.

The truth which I couldn't bring myself to tell Cat was that Tony and I had been really close for a few months last year. Cat had gone on vacation in Europe with her parents, so Tony and I spent a lot of time hanging out together. We used to go on these long walks around Cherrywood Lakes, talking about everything from music to movie stars to annoying things our parents did. Tony was into folk rock and he used to put one of his headphones in my ear so I could listen to The Lumineers with him. I wasn't as crazy about them as he was, but I did like getting up close enough to share his headphones.

Then one afternoon, we kissed. It had been my first kiss, and, I'm pretty sure, Tony's first kiss, too.

The whole truth was that I'd kissed him. He'd acted like he hadn't seen it coming, in spite of all the signals he'd been giving me in the days before. The intense gazes, the unnecessary touching – apparently all of these things had meant nothing.

After he pulled away from me, he'd wiped his lips with the back of his hand as though he'd just tasted something disgusting. He didn't hug me. He didn't tell me everything was all right. He didn't say anything at all. We walked home in silence and have barely spoken since. Even though we're neighbors, we never make eye contact anymore. There's nothing between us now. Nothing but nervous embarrassment.

That was the whole terrible truth. All I'd told Cat was that Tony and I had hung out a bit while she was away. Nothing else. I'd kept the truth from her because she had been in Europe when the kiss happened, and by the time she got back I just wanted to forget about it. Besides, she'd always said he was a muso dork.

"Keeping a secret from your best friend is hard," I whispered to Chris. "Especially when your best friend is Cat." I stared into his bright-blue eyes for a moment before continuing. "It's like she wants me to herself all the time and has to be included in every little detail of my life. Like at the grade 7 dance, when I was dancing with that cutie Stephen Brent and she came up and asked him whether it was really over with his last girlfriend. He ran a mile!"

I looked down at my pillow and then back up at Chris. "It's not that I don't totally love Cat – I do! I just don't want her nudging me in the ribs every time Tony walks past, and trying to turn it into the romance of the century. Or, worse, giving Tony a hard time for scorning me. Do you dig, Chris?" His eyes told me he understood perfectly.

I rolled onto my side, sighing. It was strange that Cat suddenly thought Tony should be my boyfriend. She'd never liked the idea of me spending any time with him before.

"I don't get it," I told Chris, looking back up at the ceiling. "She's always said he was a major nerd, but now she thinks he's a major hottie?" Not even Chris could help me make sense of that.

Now that almost a year had passed, there was more

reason than ever to keep the kiss under wraps. Cat would be outraged that I hadn't told her at the time, and I knew she'd turn it into a grand drama of betrayal.

I looked up at Chris. "She really is a drama queen," I whispered.

Then again, who was I to judge? I was having a conversation with a poster.

Chapter Two

"Oh no." Cat's mouth fell open when she saw the bulletin board the next morning.

I looked over Cat's shoulder and scanned the clutter of ads and notices stuck to the board, my eyes settling on a sign that said: AUDITIONS FOR *GLADIATOR: THE MUSICAL* WILL BE HELD IN THE AUDITORIUM THIS FRIDAY AT 3:30.

Cat was shaking her head. "*Gladiator?* The *musical?* Come *on. Gladiator's* a movie. It can't be turned into a musical. It's going to be awful! And there's only one big female part … I bet Louisa Andrews will get it. Oh, this is *so* unfair."

Louisa Andrews was the best singer at Cherrywood High. When she was only fourteen she had sung solo for the state choir.

"Maybe you can play one of the tigers," I suggested.

Cat rolled her eyes. "Thanks for the vote of confidence."

A group of older boys came striding down the hall towards us. Among them was Ollie Haas, who was a head taller than the others. They stopped when they got to the bulletin board.

"So, you girls thinking of auditioning?" Ollie asked.

I turned around, looked up at him, and melted. He was so gorgeous. Okay, not as gorgeous as Chris Hemsworth, but gorgeous enough.

"Yeah," replied Cat in a voice that was almost air.

"Actually," I croaked, "we didn't know that *Gladiator* could be turned into a musical."

"Strange choice, isn't it?"

Cat and I nodded, hanging on his every word. *Ollie Haas* was talking to *us*.

"The music's been written by a guy in your year," he continued. "You know, Anthony Rickson."

"Oh," I breathed. "Tony Rickson." Then the full force of what he was saying finally hit me. "Tony wrote the musical?"

"Yep," replied Ollie. "He wrote the songs, anyway. Pretty cool, huh?" Ollie was talking to me, but his deep blue eyes kept zeroing in on Cat.

I stood there like an idiot, my mouth opening and closing like a codfish. Grade 10s thought Tony was cool? *My* Tony? Oh, puh-*lease*! Sure, he was good at music, but he was a nerd, right? When we used to hang out, he was definitely a nerd. A nice nerd. Well, he used to be nice. But definitely he was a nerd. That was for sure.

"The guy's a genius," said one of Ollie's friends, contradicting my thoughts.

"Who's a genius?" interrupted a high-pitched female voice. It was Louisa Andrews. She smiled at Ollie and flicked her long, fox-colored hair over her shoulder. "I presume you're talking about me."

"Hey, Lou," said Ollie, laughing.

Louisa greeted the boys, but completely ignored Cat and me.

"We who are about to die, salute you!" she announced dramatically to Ollie, quoting from the movie in mock seriousness.

Ollie and his friends laughed uproariously. Cat shot me a "Kill me now" look. I rolled my eyes at her.

"These girls are auditioning too," Ollie said, gesturing to Cat and me.

Finally Louisa deigned to look at us. She narrowed her eyes at Cat. "Weren't you in the chorus last year?" she asked, looking unimpressed.

"Yes," said Cat, returning Louisa's look of contempt.

"Well, don't expect a main part this year," said Louisa. "There's only one big female part and that's Lucilla."

I remembered Lucilla from the movie. She was the Roman Emperor's daughter.

"Lucilla," repeated Ollie. "Hmmm … sounds like Louisa."

"Exactly," Louisa replied smugly.

It made me so mad that Louisa was being so charming to the boys and so rude to us. I couldn't stand it anymore. I had to stick up for Cat.

"Actually, Cat would be perfect for that part," I said. "She's part Roman, you know. Her father was born in Rome."

Louisa pursed her lips. "I think the parts will be handed out based on singing ability," she trilled, "not where your parents were born."

"Well, Cat's the best singer I know," I added. "So I guess we'll see on Friday afternoon."

"I guess we will," replied Louisa. She turned away from us, flicking her long, orange hair dramatically. It whipped across my face and I spluttered.

"See you later, guys," said Cat as we left the group. The boys' attention was on Louisa, but Ollie gave us a quick wave.

We made our way down the hall to Latin. As soon as we were inside the classroom, Cat clutched her hands to her heart. "Ollie's so hot!" she cried. "He's so gorgeous that I actually feel pain when I look at him. Right here, in my chest."

"I know what you mean," I said, remembering what I felt whenever I looked at my ceiling and saw Chris

Hemsworth's beautiful face staring down at me. "Ollie is really cute."

"We have to blitz the auditions on Friday," said Cat, sitting down at her desk.

"*We?*" I asked, sitting down next to her.

"You're coming."

"Yeah, I mean, I'll come and cheer you on, but –"

"No!" barked Cat, with force. "I need you in the musical with me. You can't leave me alone with Louisa Andrews. She'll eat me alive."

"I won't let her do that," I said, pulling my luckiest pen out of my pencil case.

"Correct," Cat replied sharply. "Because you'll be at my side at every audition, rehearsal and performance."

"But, Cat, I can't sing a note in tune. I can't be in a musical!"

"Doesn't matter. Not if you're in the chorus. You can just lip-sync."

"That's the wrong answer, Caterina-Cordelia," I said, pretending she'd wounded my feelings. "What you should have said is that I'm a really great singer."

"Okay, you're a really great singer, Ally."

We erupted with laughter.

"Care to share the joke, girls?" Mrs. Hawkins asked, picking up a stack of papers from her desk at the front of the classroom. They were our Latin tests. Cat and I stopped laughing.

"Nothing on your desk except your pen," said Mrs. Hawkins as she handed out the tests. "You have half an hour to complete this test … starting *now*."

I picked up my lucky pen. I was ready.

"You have to audition with me, Ally," hissed Cat in a stage whisper.

Ugh, I thought, trying to ignore her. She was relentless.

I took a deep breath. It was time to be honest. "I don't want to be in the musical," I whispered back.

"Of course you do!" she muttered. "We can get close to Ollie and Tony this way. It's the perfect opportunity. You'll love it." She narrowed her eyes. "And I can't audition on my own. You *have* to come."

I shot a look across at Mrs. Hawkins. She was sitting at her desk, looking down at a book she was reading.

But any minute we were going to get caught whispering during a test.

Wincing, I surrendered. "Okay," I whispered to Cat, my eyes fluttering closed with dread. "I'll do it."

It was a promise I already knew I'd regret.

Chapter Three

Mrs. Hawkins handed back our Latin tests the very next day. I stared at the red "100" written in the top right-hand corner of my test paper. I couldn't have done any better. I'd totally brained it. I guess all that studying was worth it.

"Ally Motbey, can I see you after class?" They were words that no student wanted to hear, but somehow I knew I wasn't in trouble.

"Yes, Mrs. Hawkins," I answered.

"Teacher's pet," muttered Cat.

I gave an innocent shrug. "I have no idea what she wants."

"How do you do it?" Cat whispered. "How do you get through a test as hard as that without making any mistakes?"

"The same way you get through a whole song without hitting a wrong note," I whispered back. "How did you do, anyway?"

Cat had turned her test facedown, but I could see a lot of red check marks showing through the back of the paper. "Put it this way," she said, throwing a foul look in Mrs. Hawkins's direction. "The only way to go is up."

"Same goes for my singing."

"Don't think you're getting out of the audition."

"Okay. But, I am warning you, bring your earplugs."

"I don't care if your singing breaks all the lightbulbs in the auditorium, you're coming."

I was starting to feel irritated by her comments. But when I reminded myself how much Cat wanted to be in the musical and get close to Ollie, the feeling faded. She was my best friend – of course I should help her. I figured I was probably just feeling anxious about auditioning. I really was a terrible singer.

When the bell rang at the end of class, Cat said she would wait for me in the hall. I hung back and, when the room had cleared, went to the front, where Mrs. Hawkins was sitting on the edge of her desk.

She shook her head and smiled, peering at me over the top of her reading glasses.

I smiled back. "What? What have I done?"

"Ally, you've achieved 100 percent on all three tests this year. Many students find Latin very hard, but it comes easily to you, doesn't it?" Mrs. Hawkins looked at me for a moment. "Why do you think that is?"

I shrugged. *What can I really say?* I wondered. *That I love Latin? That I find it almost as easy to read as English?* No way was I about to admit that. Saying that, even just to a teacher, would make me feel like an even bigger nerd than I know I am. A massive, supersized nerd. So I said nothing and just looked at my shoes.

"You're gifted, Ally," Mrs. Hawkins said, breaking the silence. "But I don't think you're being challenged in this class. I'd like you to attend the extension class I run for the grade 10s on Friday afternoons."

"Grade 10?" I gasped. "But I'd be way out of my depth."

"I only run an extension class for the grade 10s who are preparing to study Latin in grades 11 and 12," Mrs. Hawkins explained. "I think you're more than capable of participating at grade 10 level. And I think you'll enjoy it. At the moment, we're translating the works of the Roman poet Catullus."

Latin *and* poetry? My inner geek couldn't hide her excitement. "I'd love to join the extension class!"

Mrs. Hawkins gave me a massive smile. She looked as pleased as I felt. "I'm so glad to hear it, Ally."

She dug through her papers and passed me a permission slip for my parents to sign.

"See you here at three thirty, Friday afternoon," Mrs. Hawkins called after me, as I walked into the hall.

"See you then," I said, feeling awesome. I couldn't believe she thought I was good enough to be in an extension class with the grade 10s! I went out into the hall with a huge smile on my face.

Then I saw Cat and my smile dropped. As I watched her farther up the hall, rifling through her locker,

I remembered I was supposed to be somewhere else at three thirty on Friday afternoon — the *Gladiator* auditions. My heart sank immediately. I felt sick. *What am I going to tell her?*

Cat closed her locker and saw me coming towards her. "So?"

"So …" I replied, flatly.

"What did Hawky want? Did she say you're going to be teaching us Latin from now on?" Cat's smile was broad and mischievous. Mine felt plastered on. I knew I was going to have to either miss the Latin extension class or back out of the audition. Trying to get out of the audition would mean standing up to Cat — a terrifying prospect.

I tried to sound casual. "Oh, there's a Latin extension class she's asked me to go to. I don't know whether I'll do it … probably not, though."

Cat crinkled her face up. "*More* Latin? You're kidding, right? That's your reward for doing well?"

"I *like* Latin, Cat," I said, feeling defensive. "You know that. The same way that you love singing."

"Yeah, okay. But I don't get why you'd want to take extra classes," said Cat. "I mean, it sounds so uncool … not to mention massively nerdy."

"Ah, forget it," I said, waving my hand dismissively. I opened my locker and stared inside. "I'm not that keen anyway," I lied, chucking my books in and slamming the door shut. I *was* keen, and it was really starting to bug me that Cat didn't seem to understand that – or didn't want to.

We walked to the cafeteria together. The lunchtime line was about a mile long. Cat threw her arms up in the air dramatically. "See what happens when you stay back after class? The line turns into a monster!"

She was right. Usually we sprinted to line up the moment the lunch bell rang, elbowing grade 7 kids out of the way as we went. I walked along the line, looking for someone I knew, hoping to engage in the highly unethical practice of getting someone already in the line to buy me my lunch.

Cat was doing the same. "Look," she whispered. "There's Tony!"

"Huh?"

"Tony Rickson. Right at the front of the line!"

"No –"

"Go on, Ally," Cat said. "You guys are friends, aren't you? Ask him." She passed me a ten dollar bill. "Get me a grilled cheese sandwich and a chocolate milk."

I frowned. So now that Tony had what Cat wanted, she was happy for me to know him. Typical. I grasped the money and headed towards the front of the line. There was Tony, his shirt hanging out of his pants, his long, honey-colored hair escaping from its ponytail. Suddenly, all the embarrassment from last year flooded back, turning my face red. I really didn't want to ask him for a favor.

"Go on, Ally!" Cat shoved the heel of her hand into my back.

I staggered forward. The boy at the front of the line was just about to pay for his lunch. Tony was behind him and was going to be served next.

I tapped Tony on the shoulder. "Hi there," I said, waving the money in his direction.

"Hey," he said absently, glancing at the money. He looked confused.

The lunch lady rapped on the top of the counter impatiently. "What can I get you?"

"Um …" Tony looked at her then back at me and shrugged.

I opened my mouth to speak, but nothing came out. I just couldn't ask him. It was too awkward. He turned back to the cafeteria lady and ordered his lunch. I just stood there like an idiot, staring at his back, which was a lot broader than I remembered.

Maybe Cat was right. Maybe Tony Rickson was turning into a hunk.

"What's wrong with you today, Ally?" Cat asked, when we'd finally bought our lunches and were sitting on the grass by the art rooms.

"What do you mean?"

"Well, since when have you been too shy to push into the cafeteria line?"

I bit into my ham sandwich and chewed for a long time. "Tony's just my dorky neighbor. He's not my friend, Cat. I didn't want to ask him."

"And I didn't want to wait in the cafeteria line for twenty minutes," Cat shot back.

"I'm sorry, Cat. Okay? If it'd been anyone other than him, I would have been fine." I took another bite of the ham sandwich – a huge one this time.

Cat shook her head, looking serious. "You guys are going to have to sort out your differences before the rehearsals for *Gladiator* start."

Gladiator! The scene at the cafeteria had made me forget all about my double booking on Friday afternoon. How was I going to juggle a Latin class with Mrs. Hawkins and an audition in the auditorium? Ordinarily it wouldn't have been a difficult choice. I knew where my talents lay, and that certainly wasn't in the auditorium. But I'd promised Cat. How could I leave her to fend for herself against a trilling, flame-haired grade 10 witch like Louisa Andrews? Cat would never get close to Ollie with Louisa making fun of her every move. Besides, if I backed out now, I was fairly sure that Cat would hold it against me for the rest of my life – no exaggeration.

On the other hand, I really wanted to go to the Latin class. It was a beautiful language, with so much interesting literature. The extension class was a great opportunity – I didn't want to miss out. And I didn't want to disappoint Mrs. Hawkins, either. She was a great teacher, and she really seemed to see potential in me.

I wondered if maybe it was time I said no to Cat and did something under my own steam – for the first time ever.

Sometime before Friday I was going to have to make a decision.

"Ally?" Cat waved her hand up and down in front of my face. "Babe, you are a total space cadet today. Are you sick?"

"No. I'm okay." I blinked quickly and smiled, then scrunched up my empty sandwich wrapper and threw it in a nearby trash can. "Let's go back to the cafeteria for an ice cream."

"Okay," said Cat. "But this time, I'll do the pushing in. I'm not going to the back of the line again." She linked her arm in mine, and we walked back to the cafeteria.

When I got home that afternoon I flopped onto my bed, feeling emotionally exhausted. I looked up at Chris Hemsworth.

In the poster, he was shirtless, crouching on one knee with his square chin resting in his hand. He was staring at the camera, his brow slightly furrowed in a serious, challenging look. Chris was decisive. Chris was tough. Chris knew everything.

"Chris," I said. "What should I do?"

I practically jumped out of my skin when someone knocked on my door.

"Ally?" It was Mum.

"Yeah?"

"Have you got someone in there?" she asked through the door.

"No. Of course not."

She opened the door and looked in, then smiled. "I thought I heard voices," she said. "Tony Rickson's here to see you."

I sat bolt upright. "What?"

"He's at the front door."

"What? Right now?" I jumped off my bed and headed for the front door throwing my head back for a final glance at Chris. *Wish me luck*, I mouthed silently.

Tony was standing on the front porch. I didn't invite him in.

"Hey," he said, looking up from his shoes.

"Hi," I said, finding it difficult to believe that this was the "cool genius" behind the apparently amazing *Gladiator: The Musical.*

"Um … I guess I just wanted to apologize."

"Oh?" *Finally*, I thought, with a little tremor of excitement. *He's finally going to apologize for leaving me twisting in the wind after our terrible kiss.*

"Yeah, I … ah … didn't realize … um …" He trailed off in a volley of ums and ahs. I couldn't see this guy with a speaking role in a play. Lucky he could write songs.

"Spit it out, Tony," I said snippily, gaining confidence as his seemed to fade.

"Well ..." He gave an awkward chuckle, then looked up at me again. "I'm sorry that I didn't realize you wanted me to buy you something in the cafeteria today. When I thought about it later, I worked it out."

"That's okay, Tony," I replied, trying to sound nonchalant. I was disappointed, but I didn't let it show. "Is there anything else?"

"No." He gulped. "I mean, um, I don't think so. Sorry."

I was relieved when I heard Mum calling me to dinner. Then she bustled up behind me in the hallway and stuck her head around the front door. "Would you like to stay for dinner, Tony?" she asked.

I jumped in before the invitation could be accepted. "He was just leaving."

Tony nodded. "See you later, Ally. Nice to see you, Mrs. Motbey."

I shut the door quickly.

"Well, it's no wonder you two aren't friends anymore, if that's how you treat him! That was very rude, Ally," Mum said as we sat down to dinner.

"What?" I blinked at her, as if I had no idea what she was talking about. "I didn't invite him over here. He just showed up unannounced."

"Maybe he's trying to rekindle the friendship. Ever thought of that?"

"No," I answered, feeling embarrassed and grumpy.

I sat down at the dinner table glaring at the sausages and potatoes on my plate, as if they were the ones weighing in on issues they knew nothing about. I mean, what could my mother possibly understand about my problems? Tony was the least of them.

My phone beeped with a message. I pulled it out of my pocket. It was from Cat.

Let's practice for the audition at lunch tomorrow. You'll be amazing. So excited! xx

All through dinner I turned over my big dilemma in my mind. What was I going to choose? The *Gladiator* audition or the Latin extension class?

If I went to the audition, I'd humiliate myself in front of everyone, and even if I could somehow pull it off I would be stuck working with Tony. But if I blew it off, I'd be leaving Cat in the lurch – something she'd probably never forgive me for.

But I didn't want to miss out on the Latin class either. It was a *grade 10* extension class! That wasn't an opportunity I could throw away without a second thought. Latin was my favorite subject. What was I going to do?

If you think Ally should go to the musical audition with Cat, go to page 43.

If you think Ally should join the Latin extension class, go to page 70.

Ally GOES to the MUSICAL
AUDITION with Cat

Chapter Four

"Okay, Ally. I want you to sing the note I'm playing. Don't just sing some random note."

It was lunchtime. Cat and I were in the auditorium, both perched cross-legged on the edge of the stage. Cat had her guitar balanced in her lap, and she was looking super serious. This would be her last opportunity to knock my singing into shape before the audition. "Ready?" she asked.

I wriggled and sat up straighter. "Yep, ready."

Cat plucked a string of her guitar, then looked at me expectantly.

I opened my mouth and sang.

"No, Ally, that's not it." I detected a tinge of exasperation in my friend's voice.

"Cat," I said, sounding whiny and feeling over it, "I haven't been singing random notes. I've been trying to sing the notes you've been playing."

"But can't you hear that what's coming out of your mouth is nothing like what's coming from my guitar?" She looked baffled.

I shrugged. I really couldn't hear it.

"Look, Ally. Close your eyes. *Listen* to the note. Then hum it. You only have to hum. I'm not expecting Edith Piaf."

"Who's Edith Piaf?"

"Only one of the greatest singers of the twentieth century," she said, like I was an idiot. "But forget about her. Just hum *one note* in tune."

"But I have been." There was an uncomfortable pause. "Haven't I?"

Cat shook her head sadly.

"Maybe your guitar's out of tune," I suggested. "Ever thought of that?"

"Look," Cat said, gazing at me with pity. "I don't want to use the word 'foghorn' but –"

"Hey!" Even though I was slightly offended, I started laughing and then couldn't stop.

Cat gave me a wry smile, and then broke into giggles too.

"What's going on here?" Standing in the doorway to the auditorium was Ollie Haas, doing a very convincing "grumpy teacher" impression. As he walked towards us, I saw that he was with another guy, who was wearing a private school uniform.

Cat and I fell silent immediately.

"Practicing for the audition on Friday?" asked Ollie.

Cat and I looked at each other blankly. I wasn't sure what to say. Would it be too uncool to admit that we were making an effort?

"I-I'm practicing," I stuttered. "Cat's helping me."

Cat clutched her guitar to her body. It looked like she was trying to protect herself from Ollie's jaw-dropping gorgeousness.

"So you play the guitar, huh?" he asked Cat. "Me too."

Cat just nodded.

"What kind of music are you into?"

Cat gripped her guitar for dear life. "Oh, anything and everything."

"Do you write your own songs?"

She seemed to relax a bit. "Yeah, I've written a few," she said, smiling. "What about you?"

I sat in awe as Cat and Ollie struck up a real conversation. Cat was doing a great job of playing it cool.

"Mind if we stay and listen?" Ollie dropped into a seat near the stage. His friend grinned and sat down next to him.

Cat looked to me, her eyebrows raised encouragingly.

I wasn't so sure. The last thing I wanted to do was spoil an opportunity for Cat to spend time with Ollie, but if I really did sound like a foghorn …

"Well," I said. "We were about to wrap it up, weren't we, Cat?"

"No, no!" said Ollie. "Keep going. We want to hear you sing."

I snorted and then covered my mouth with my hand. How embarrassing to snort in front of His Royal Gorgeousness! That was hardly going to win any points for Cat.

"What is it?" Ollie asked.

"I can't actually sing," I blurted out.

"Well, don't say that in front of Mrs. Carey's son," Ollie said with mock horror.

His private school friend grinned at me.

I looked at him, feeling mortified. "You're Mrs. Carey's son?"

Mrs. Carey was head of music at Cherrywood High, and she always directed the school musical. I'd heard she was really tough on her performers – apparently she'd made the male lead cry during rehearsal a couple of years ago! Mrs. Carey would also have the final say on casting, and now I'd gone and admitted to her son that I couldn't sing. What a disaster.

I was beginning to seriously regret agreeing to try out for the musical instead of going to my Latin extension class. The way things were going I'd probably end up missing out on the musical *and* Latin class.

"I'm Paul, by the way," the guy in the private school uniform said.

"Ally," I replied in a small voice.

"Don't worry, Ally," said Paul. "I'll let Mum be the judge on Friday. She wouldn't listen to me anyway." He beamed at me. Even though he had braces, I could still see that he had a cute smile.

"Is that a Penscombe uniform?" I asked. Penscombe was the most exclusive private school in our area.

He nodded, and then smirked. "Please don't hold that against me."

"I *would* hold it against him if I were you," said Ollie. "He's just as stuck-up as everyone else at that school. Don't let him fool you."

The boys laughed in the kind of confident guffaw I'd heard the older boys at school use around each other. I started to relax. Paul and Ollie were fun – and really nice! – and nowhere near as scary as I'd first thought.

Cat and I exchanged looks. I could tell that she was enjoying the company of these boys as much as I was.

"So what are you doing here … I mean, at Cherry-wood High?" I asked Paul.

"Mum's asked me to help with the musical," he explained. "I'm going to take care of the sound and lighting. Ollie's showing me around so I can get a feel for the place. You know, the acoustics and stuff."

"The acoustics are great in here," said Cat, pointing upward. "I think it's the vaulted ceiling. It makes anyone sound good." She shot me a cheeky look. "Well, *almost* anyone."

"Come on, girls," said Ollie. "We can take it. Give us your worst."

Just when I was starting to panic, I had a stroke of genius. "Cat, why don't you sing something? What about that song by Gotye?"

"Yeah, I know Gotye!" said Paul. "How about *Somebody That I Used to Know*?"

Cat smiled, and her dimples went deep like they always did when she was embarrassed in a good way.

"Yes!" I cheered. "You must have played that song a million times, Cat."

Cat repositioned her guitar on her lap and strummed over the strings to make sure it was in tune. The boys gave whoops and a short round of applause before I raised my finger to my lips and cut them off. Then she played the opening chords of the song perfectly.

When she started singing, I closed my eyes, amazed as usual by the way she managed to match her voice to the pitch and rhythm of the guitar – or was it the other way around? I didn't know how she coaxed such beautiful tones from that wooden box. In my hands, it just made noise.

The other thing I loved about Cat's performances was that she never tried to mimic the voice of the artist whose song she was singing. She always made the music her own. Her sweet, rich voice rolled over the edges of Gotye's melody like maple syrup. It was beautiful. How could they even consider giving the main part in *Gladiator* to anyone but Cat?

I opened my eyes when I heard Ollie singing along in a lower register. He and Cat were gazing at each other as they sang. It was cute, but cringeworthy. When

I looked at Paul, he was already looking at me. He grinned and I shrugged.

Cat was belting out the final phrases of the song, holding the last note for longer than Ollie could, when a loud bang broke the spell. All eyes shot to the auditorium doors, which Louisa Andrews had just slammed behind her.

"Hey, Lou," called Ollie in a friendly voice.

Ugh! I thought. Why couldn't he see what a piece of work she was?

"*There* you are," cooed Louisa. "I've been looking *everywhere* for you boys."

Ollie and Paul stood and turned to Louisa. Cat and I rolled our eyes. Louisa opened the carton of coffee-flavored milk she'd been shaking and shoved a straw into it. She sipped on it delicately as she approached the stage taking tiny princess steps.

"Cat was just serenading us," said Paul.

"Cat?" Louisa sniggered. "I thought I heard a cat being strangled." She blinked innocently at Cat. "Oh, was that you?"

"And me," added Ollie with a chuckle. He was certainly taking the insults better than Cat, whose face was like storm clouds gathering.

"I don't sound like a cat being strangled," Cat said in a low voice.

Louisa's lips spread in a mean smile. "All right then, what *do* you sound like?"

"She sounds like Edith Piaf," I jumped in. "And if you don't know who Edith Piaf is, then you don't know much about music." I uncrossed my legs and hopped off the stage. "Come on, Cat."

Cat quickly put her guitar in its case and zipped it up. I picked up what remained of my sandwich and hurled it past Louisa to the trash can near the stage. Incredibly, it landed where it was supposed to.

"She shoots, she scores!" cried Paul.

I gave him a little smile as we walked past them. Cat glared at the floor.

"See ya Friday, girls!" Ollie shouted after us. He seemed perfectly cheerful, as if he hadn't even noticed how badly Louisa had put down Cat.

I didn't want to destroy my best friend's illusions, but I was beginning to think there wasn't a great deal between Ollie Haas's ears. He was like a cocker spaniel – determined to be happy no matter what.

As we were walking up to the double doors, we heard Louisa's soprano voice fill the auditorium. The words she was singing – and they weren't easy to make out through her exaggerated operatic vibrato – seemed to be French.

"Oh, you've got to be kidding!" muttered Cat, rolling her eyes at me.

"What? What is it?"

"She's singing *La Vie en Rose* by Edith Piaf."

"Geez … just to show us that she knows who Edith Piaf is." I shook my head in disbelief as I pulled the double doors shut behind us. "Honestly, Cat, how are you going to stand being in the musical with that girl?"

"I don't know. Let's hope she gets laryngitis in the next forty-eight hours." Cat linked her arm in mine. We set off down the hall towards our English class. "But you'll be by my side the whole time, right?"

I nodded. "You know, she's not even that great," I said. And I really meant it. To me, Louisa's voice sounded desperate and shrill compared to Cat's.

My best friend sighed. "Thanks, Ally. But I think we should admit it when someone's good. I mean, Louisa Andrews may not be a very nice person, but she does have an outstanding voice."

I shrugged. "She sounds like a constipated canary to me. Then again, I sound like a foghorn, so who am I to talk?"

Cat grinned. "Did I say 'foghorn'? I meant 'French horn.'"

"You lie about as well as I sing, Caterina-Cordelia."

"Do you think our session helped?" Cat asked doubtfully.

"Helped what?"

"Helped *you*, of course!"

I shook my head gloomily. Ever since I'd sung my first "note" in the auditorium, I'd been wishing I could do the Latin extension class instead. "I'm beyond help," I explained. "I'm going to crash and burn in that audition."

"I hope no one gets hurt."

"Just my pride." I paused, taking a deep breath, wondering whether it was worth one last crack at trying to wriggle out of the audition. "Cat, I don't think I'm going to be much use to you at the audition. I was thinking … maybe … you'd be better off without me. Singing just isn't my thing. I'm probably not going to be chosen for the musical anyway. And I already kind of promised Mrs. Hawkins that I'd show up to the Latin extension class."

Cat's face hardened as I tripped and stammered through my excuses. I tried to look away, but she herded my eyes back to hers.

"Best friends back each other up," she said, laying a hand on my shoulder. "Don't they? Otherwise what's the point of having a best friend?"

"Um … yeah," I agreed slowly. "What's the point?" Was Cat threatening to dump me if I didn't do what she wanted?

She squeezed my shoulder and smiled. It was as if she hadn't heard a single word I'd said.

"I want you to know how much I appreciate you *keeping your promise* on this."

"I know," I said. "But —"

"I owe you one."

"I know that too."

It was nice to be appreciated – sort of. I couldn't help thinking that if Cat *really* appreciated me, she wouldn't have ignored my wishes.

Chapter Five

That afternoon, Cat and I took the bus home together as usual. We got off at Cat's stop, dropped her stuff on her doorstep and then she walked me through the park. When we got to my house, we were right in the middle of an argument about what Ollie's best feature was, so I dumped my bag on my front lawn and we walked back through the park to her house.

"You know what I love even more than his butt?" I didn't really care about Ollie's butt, but I was having fun trying to bait Cat.

"His eyes?"

"Nope." I paused for effect, waiting until Cat was

really hanging. "His mind."

"Yeah," said Cat, nodding slowly. "I love his mind, too. He doesn't seem to have any bad thoughts."

"I don't think he has many thoughts, period."

I glanced at Cat and watched her face change as she realized I was teasing her.

"You don't think he's smart?" she asked cautiously.

I shrugged. "Do you?"

"I don't know. Not really, I guess." A smile spread slowly across her face. "But, Ally, he *is* a nice guy."

"He is super nice," I agreed.

"So, stop trying to make me feel shallow for liking him. And don't pretend you aren't just as knocked out by him as I am." She linked her arm through mine. "Oh, sorry, I forgot, you've only got eyes for Chris Hemsworth. I'm sure *Chris* has an IQ of 250 and can recite the periodic table backward."

We both cracked up laughing. This silly banter was why it took us so long to get home in the afternoon. I didn't even mind that Cat was making fun of Chris.

"That Paul guy was cute," I said a bit shyly.

"Yeah," agreed Cat. "I can't believe he's Mrs. Carey's son. I mean, she's such a dragon and he's so friendly." She nudged me with her shoulder, smirking. "But what about Tony?"

"What about him?" I bumped her back, a bit harder.

"You need to get some experience with a real, live guy," said Cat, who – after a kiss with a boy at ski camp – had appointed herself the grand high priestess of experience.

I looked sideways at her and shrugged.

"I mean, you've never even held someone's hand," she added.

"I've held yours."

"I don't count," Cat said with a smirk.

I thought about my secret kissing incident with Tony. I wanted to blurt it out to Cat then and there, and wipe the condescending smile off her face. But I knew it would end up making trouble between us. Anyway, we'd arrived at her front door and I could see Gina watching us through the blinds in the family room.

Cat spotted her too, and groaned. "I guess this is

where I get off."

Gina opened the front door. "Come on now," she said to Cat. Then she smiled at me. "Hi, Ally."

"Hi, Gina. I've delivered her safely home again."

On the way back home, I felt a bit lonely without Cat. Sometimes it felt good to walk by myself and clear my mind of all the chatter and clutter before I got home. But this afternoon I just missed her and wished we could have kept chatting.

By the time I reached the other end of the park and crossed the road, the streetlights were on. As I turned the corner into our street, I saw Tony Rickson. He was walking towards me from the other end of the street. As I approached my house and he approached his, I realized we were going to have to talk to each other again. I groaned.

I looked at the sidewalk right up until the last moment, then lifted my head to look him in the eye. He must have been doing the same thing because we almost slammed into each other.

"Hey, Ally."

"Hi."

I wanted the conversation to end right there. He probably did, too. But I decided I wasn't going to leave it at that. It would only make it harder to talk to each other once the musical rehearsals started – assuming I made it into the chorus. I was determined to force out some conversation, no matter how awkward it was. Plus, if I was completely honest, I did feel bad about being so rude to Tony when he'd come over last night to apologize.

"So …" I began weakly. "Did you catch the four-thirty bus?"

"The ten past five, actually."

I looked at my watch and shook my head. "Wow! It's nearly five thirty." There was a long, uncomfortable pause. I tried to think of something to say. "It's getting dark early, isn't it?"

"Yeah."

"So where have you been? I mean, if you're coming home so late."

"Oh, you know, stuff for the musical. Mrs. Carey's

son's doing the sound and lighting, so I had a meeting with him about my, er, my vision for *Gladiator*."

"You mean Paul?"

"Yeah. Do you know him?"

"Not really. I just met him today."

"He's cool. I mean, I know he goes to Penscombe and his mother is Mrs. Carey and everything, but he's still pretty cool." Then Tony actually smiled. A big smile. A real one.

It was a smile you only got to see if he felt comfortable with you. I hadn't seen him smile like that for ages. It made me feel strange and wistful and sad, all at the same time. All these smiles and words after a year of nothing — it was as though we'd slipped into an alternate reality. Was this the "cool" Tony that Ollie and his friends had been talking about?

"So you're going to audition for *Gladiator*?" he asked.

"Well, Cat's auditioning ... I'll just be happy to get into the chorus."

"You still have to audition to get into the chorus."

"Yeah, I know. I'm terrified."

"How come?"

The conversation was flowing more easily now. It was just a shame that the topic sucked. I sighed. "I'm just not a great singer."

"Not many people are naturally great singers. But everyone can improve with training."

I snorted, and then grinned. "You'd think so, wouldn't you?"

"Why? Aren't you getting any better?"

I shook my head.

"Do you sing along to the songs on the radio?"

"Yeah, but I still can't sing in tune."

Tony nodded slowly. Then his forehead furrowed. "So how come you're auditioning for the musical?" he asked, looking confused.

For a terrible moment I thought he might be under the impression that *he* was the reason I wanted to do the musical. Nothing – *nothing* – could be further from the truth. I was doing it because Cat needed me. Because I had promised her.

"Well, just because I can't sing, doesn't mean I don't

like music. And besides, Cat wants me there for moral support."

He grinned and I noticed how much nicer his face was when he was happy. He'd also pushed his hair out of his eyes, which were bright and attentive instead of darting around nervously.

I'd honestly forgotten what I'd seen in Tony for that short time last year, but now I was starting to remember. Not that I was having *those* feelings. No, I was definitely still uncomfortable around him.

"Sounds like you could use some coaching," he said.

I shrugged. "That's what Cat's been trying to do."

"I could train you," offered Tony.

There was a weird jump in my stomach when he said this. I tried to ignore it. I was definitely not having *feelings* for Tony.

I thought about his offer for a moment. The auditions were the day after tomorrow, so I did need urgent help. On the other hand, what was the point? I was so far from being able to sing a note in tune. There was no way anyone was going to turn me into Edith

Piaf in the next two days. I didn't know what to say.

But Tony hadn't given up yet. "We could go through the song you'll have to sing at the audition."

"Nobody knows what that is, though."

"I do," said Tony. "I wrote it." He flicked his hair out of his eyes and met my gaze.

My stomach lurched again. I searched my feelings. Was I nervous about singing? Or was it Tony? I couldn't find the answer. I opened my mouth and closed it. Then I opened it again. "Um …"

"Come on, Ally. It's not a complicated piece. And knowing the song will be a big advantage."

Suddenly I felt a wave of irritation run through me. Who did Tony think he was, offering me singing lessons out of the blue like this? Did he really think he could help me when Cat couldn't?

To be honest, I was still pretty mad at him. He'd really hurt me last year, and I still didn't understand what had gone wrong. Even so, something inside me urged me to say yes. Tony was a genius – and he'd be a great teacher. But I kept shaking my head. Being coached by Tony would be too bizarre, wouldn't it?

A screen door opened and we both looked towards my house. It was Mum.

"Ally, it's almost dark. And it's freezing."

"*Okay*, Mum."

"Who are you talking to?" she asked.

"It's just Tony," I said.

"Hi, Mrs. Motbey," he said politely.

"Hello, Tony. Nice to see you. I'm sorry, but can I have her back, please?" Then Mum went inside, apparently oblivious to the momentousness of Tony and me actually talking.

"I have to go," I said.

"Let me know what you decide," said Tony. "You could come over after dinner tonight."

"Maybe," I said noncommittally, stepping out of the light cast by the streetlight and walking towards our front door. I was trying to play it cool, but my stomach was still doing flips.

"Nice talking to you, Ally," he called after me.

When I got inside, I went straight to my room to

consult Chris Hemsworth.

"Chris," I whispered. "What should I do?"

Chris looked down at me wisely. He seemed to be telling me that I already knew the answer. I tried to consider the options calmly.

I needed help with the audition, there was no doubt about that. My singing really sucked, and without coaching I was going to humiliate myself on Friday afternoon.

But letting Tony coach me would mean opening myself up to him again. When I was singing, I had no confidence in myself. I was totally exposed. Did I really want to put myself in that position *again*?

But that wasn't the only thing bothering me about Tony's offer. How would I explain a private coaching session with Tony to Cat? She hadn't liked it when he and I were friends before – even though now she seemed to want me to date him. It all just seemed too messy. Maybe I'd have to keep it from her. *Another* secret. I hated the idea of keeping more secrets from Cat. On the other hand, I couldn't afford to bomb out at the audition. Where would I be then? Cat would be furious with me. And I would have blown off the Latin class for nothing. What was I going to do?

If you think Ally should accept Tony's offer, go to page 100.

If you think Ally should refuse Tony's offer, go to page 132.

Ally JOINS the Latin extension class

Chapter Four

"I'm looking for books by Catullus," I told Mrs. Gray, the school librarian.

She looked at me blankly, her hands poised over the keyboard. "Is Catullus her first name or her surname?" she asked.

I hid a smile. Sometimes I forgot that not everybody loved poets as much as I did. "I think that *he* is known by his surname only. He was a Roman poet."

"Just Catullus?"

"Yeah."

Without a smile, Mrs. Gray typed something on the keyboard and stared at the computer screen.

It was Thursday and I was getting ready for the Latin extension class the next afternoon. Mrs. Hawkins had said that we didn't need to prepare, but I wanted to get up close and personal with Catullus in advance. Being a grade 9 in a grade 10 extension class, I was bound to know less Latin than the other students in the class, but I was determined not to look like an idiot in front of them.

I had done some research and found that Catullus had written sixty-eight poems. I planned to read the English translations of all of them before the class.

"Looks like we have a Catullus anthology," said Mrs. Gray, gesturing to the back of the library with a vague wave of her hand. "It's in the poetry section. Look for 874.01 CAT." She wrote the call number down on a little square of paper and gave it to me.

"Thanks, Mrs. Gray. I'll check it out."

I scanned the shelves of the poetry section, but I couldn't find the book. In fact, I couldn't find anything by Catullus. I went back to the beginning of the shelf and started again. Squinting at the call numbers, I was hating Dewey, or whoever it was that invented this ridiculous library classification system.

"Come on, Dewey Decimal!" I whispered. "What have you done with Catullus?"

"It's right here," said a calm male voice that seemed to come out of nowhere.

I froze. I obviously wasn't expecting an answer. Had the bookshelves started speaking? Or was it the ghost of Dewey Decimal coming to wreak his revenge on me?

"Where?" I asked timidly, wondering whether Cherrywood High was about to go all Hogwarts on me.

Two bespectacled blue eyes appeared in a gap between the books.

"Oh!" Surprised, I jumped backward, tripped over my own feet and ended up sprawled on the floor.

The owner of the blue eyes bounded around the side of the bookshelf. "I am *so* sorry," he said. He leaned over and offered me his hand. "I really didn't mean for that to happen."

I took a good look at him as he pulled me to my feet. He was a grade 10 boy I'd seen around school but had never spoken to. He was very, very tall and he looked bookish but handsome, in a short-back-and-sides kind of way. Behind his glasses, I could see his surprised blue eyes were taking *me* in, too. We stared at one another for a few moments before I finally let go of his hand.

"I'm James," he said confidently. "James Whisker." He smiled and I couldn't help but notice how straight and white his teeth were.

"I'm Ally."

"Ally Motbey?"

"Um, yes. How did you know that?" I was surprised. Most of the students at Cherrywood High acted like people in the lower grades didn't even exist.

"Mrs. Hawkins talks about you all the time."

"Mrs. Hawkins? Why?"

James grinned. "Every time we complain that something's difficult in Latin, she says, 'Come on, *discipuli*, Ally Motbey from grade 9 could do this!' It drives us nuts."

I felt a blush come on. I had no idea what to say. I just mumbled, "Sorry."

"Don't worry. It's not your fault you're a Latin prodigy."

I covered my mouth. "I'm not a prodigy. I can't believe she talks about me in your class." I shook my head. "How embarrassing."

"Take it as a compliment, Ally."

There was a brief, awkward silence. I felt a little mesmerized by those blue eyes. Then we both started talking at once. "So – " We stopped, and James smiled. I chuckled uncomfortably.

"So, you're looking for the Catullus anthology?" James continued. "Wait here." He disappeared behind the bookshelf again and returned a few seconds later with a thick, hardcover book. He handed it to me.

"Aren't you going to borrow it?" I asked.

"Nah, I was just browsing through it on the couch. I thought I'd better find out what Catullus was all about before Friday."

"Oh, so you're in the extension class!" I cried, much too excitedly. "I'm going to be in it too."

"I know," said James with a shrewd grin. "We're

under strict instructions not to leave you out."

"Oh," I mumbled, holding the brick-like book in front of my face. James pushed it down gently.

"That's better," he said, smiling. "You don't have to prepare for the class, you know."

"That's what Mrs. Hawkins said," I admitted. "But I feel like I'm out of my depth."

"Ally Motbey out of her depth?" teased James. "I didn't think it was possible!"

I tucked the book under my arm. "I'll just have a quick look," I assured him.

James folded his arms and looked down at me over his glasses with mock disapproval. "You know you're going to make the rest of us look bad, Ally," he teased.

I shook my head and blushed again.

James grinned his hypnotic white-toothed grin. "See you on Friday."

"Yeah, see you," I croaked.

Clutching the Catullus anthology close, I joined the line at the checkout counter. While I was waiting, James breezed past with his backpack slung over his shoulder, playfully tugging my braid on the way out. He grinned back at me as he left.

"Hey!" I said, spinning around.

Mrs. Gray gave me a sharp look.

"He pulled my hair," I explained, reaching back to touch my braid where James had tugged it. "Does he come in here often?"

"Almost every day," she replied snippily. "He never pulls anyone's hair."

I laid the anthology on the counter. Mrs. Gray looked at it as though it was a bit of roadkill.

"I just want to borrow this, please?" I asked.

"Well, you can't," she replied. "It's a reference book. It has to stay in the library." She smiled at me smugly.

Scowling, I scooped the book up under my arm once again, and headed back to the shelves. I considered sitting and reading the book for a while, but then the end of lunch bell rang and I had to put it back on the shelf. I would have to look up the poems on the Internet when I got home. I felt *so* unprepared.

I couldn't help imagining the grade 10 Latin class

laughing about the "grade 9 Latin prodigy." That thought just made me even more nervous about going to the extension class. I started wondering if perhaps I had made the wrong choice, that perhaps I should have agreed to audition for the musical after all.

At least then I would have had Cat, instead of 874.01 CAT, which was no help at all. On the other hand, I wouldn't have had a cute grade 10 boy help me to my feet and pull on my braid, would I?

Chapter Five

"What do you think's going to happen on *Supermodel Scout* tonight?" I asked Cat as we boarded the bus that afternoon.

Cat shrugged. "The usual, I suppose," she replied coldly.

Being cold wasn't Cat's natural state, but in the two days since I'd told her I wasn't doing the audition, she had definitely been giving me the cold shoulder.

Supermodel Scout was our favorite reality TV show. We'd watched last year's season religiously and the new season was just about to start. I'd thought it was something I could get Cat excited about. I was wrong.

"So Eva Mendel isn't doing it this year," I persisted.

Cat looked at me blankly. "Doing what?"

"Come on, Cat … she isn't hosting *Supermodel Scout*."

Cat shrugged again, and looked out the window as the bus pulled out from the curb. "Oh well."

"Linda Paice is taking her spot." I waited for a reaction. There wasn't one. I kept trying. "Linda Paice. She's gorgeous, don't you think? And still so down-to-earth."

Another shrug. Her shoulders were going to fall off at this rate. "Maybe."

Getting Cat back to normal was turning out to be harder than I'd expected. When I'd told her, she'd sworn she didn't mind that I wasn't going to be in the musical, but I didn't need to be a mind reader to get that was a total lie. It was obvious she minded a lot. She could hardly even look at me.

Next, I tried talking about Ollie. Under normal circumstances, the topic would have seen her in a state of high excitement, but not today. Cat was not interested.

"When he hears you sing," I said, "any thoughts of Louisa Andrews are going to fly straight out of his mind." But my compliment didn't hit the mark.

"He's heard me sing, Ally. We were in the musical together last year."

"But you were in the chorus then. How could he have picked out your voice?"

Cat gave a dismissive wave of her hand.

I figured there was no point asking her what was wrong. I already knew. I'd broken my promise, and now I was paying the price. Nevertheless, I was getting pretty fed up with talking to a brick wall for days on end.

Usually Cat took up all of my time, so I didn't really need to talk to anyone else. I knew that everyone at school saw us as an exclusive pair. Now that I thought about it, it was actually a little bit annoying. There were some other girls in my classes who I would like to get to know better, but Cat always seemed to want me to herself. Right at that moment though, sitting on the bus, the opposite seemed to be true. I was missing my best friend.

I wanted to tell Cat how nervous I was about joining the grade 10 Latin class, and how I'd made a fool of myself in the library that afternoon. I wanted to gossip about James Whisker and how cute he was, even though he wore glasses. But now all those things just seemed like reminders of how I'd abandoned Cat and the auditions.

I was also pretty sure that Cat didn't like the idea of me joining a special class. It wasn't because she didn't care. She *did* care, and that was the problem. She hated it when people wouldn't do what she wanted them to do. She thought Latin was dorky and a waste of time, and was mad that I didn't agree with her. When I told her I was definitely going to join the class, she just said, "You're going full dork on me, Ally." Then she had laughed, as if it was just a joke. But her comment had stung.

I was determined to break down the wall between Cat and me. When the bus arrived at her stop, I got off as well and walked her to her house.

Gina was in the front garden raking leaves. "Hi, Ally," she said. "Are you nervous about the musical audition too?"

I opened my mouth to explain, but Cat jumped in. "Oh, Ally's not auditioning, Mum. She's been picked for some *brainiac* whiz kid Latin class."

"Mrs. Hawkins really wants me to do it," I tried to explain to Gina. "I wanted to do the musical with Cat, but —"

BANG! Cat had gone inside and slammed the door behind her.

Gina rolled her eyes. "She's been really moody lately."

"Should I go after her, do you think?"

"If you like. But she probably just needs some time alone with her headphones, to be honest."

I considered going up to Cat's room, but there was a little voice in the back of my head reminding me how little time I had to search for Catullus's poetry on the Internet.

"I think I'll just go," I told Gina.

"I'm sure she'll be a new person once this audition's over. She just puts so much pressure on herself."

I walked home through the park feeling pretty

rotten. The Latin extension class had seemed like a great opportunity, but I was feeling so guilty for leaving Cat in the lurch. She'd never been so icy and distant with me before. Sure, we'd had arguments, but they'd always burned out quickly, leaving us better friends than ever. This time felt different.

I couldn't help thinking that it was all my fault. This time I had chosen to do something different and not just go along with Cat's plans. *If I'd just agreed to do the musical she wouldn't be treating me like this*, I thought. But was that a good way for best friends to be? I couldn't decide.

I was about four minutes from home, wondering whether our friendship was going to survive the strain, when it started raining. *Not a good omen*, I thought. I ran the rest of the way home, wishing I'd just stayed on the bus until my stop.

An hour later I was sitting at the computer in the study.

I'd found a website with an English translation of all Catullus's poems. Some of the poems, like the love poems to his girlfriend, were sweet and beautiful. But others – most of them, in fact – were crude and insulting, and very funny. I'd never thought of the Romans as having a good sense of humor.

Catullus liked to make fun of people in the meanest possible way. There were a bunch of poems about his foul-smelling friends. In a poem called *Odorous: To Rufus*, he accused Rufus of having armpits like a wild goat! And in another poem, he compared someone's face to a mule's bottom …

Wowsers, I thought. *You wouldn't have wanted to get on the wrong side of Catullus*. His enemies had been dead for over two thousand years and here I was, reading about their bad breath and BO! And I thought falling over in the library was embarrassing …

Most of the poems were short and I managed to get through all of them before it was time for dinner.

Mum and Dad were distracted, talking about the cockroach problem they had just noticed in our kitchen.

But Catullus phrases and images kept popping into my head as I ate, and my parents finally noticed I was being quieter than usual.

"What are you smiling about?" asked Dad during dessert.

"Oh, nothing really," I said. "I was just thinking about something funny I read on the Internet."

"I hope you haven't been looking at inappropriate websites," he said.

Mum scoffed. "When I poked my head in she was looking at Roman poetry. Hardly inappropriate!"

Mum and Dad both laughed, and I just smiled.

After dinner, I called Cat, but she didn't answer. I had just wanted to tell her about the clever, vulgar poems. Instead, I took a photo of Chris Hemsworth and sent it with a text:

Break a leg @ the audition tomorrow. Love Chris. PS Ally says stop looking at me – I'm hers.

I waited all night for her reply, but it never came.

Chapter Six

On Friday I tried to get Cat to come to the library at lunchtime, but she wasn't interested. "I only read Latin under extreme pressure," she said. "I would never do it *voluntarily*."

"But this is different," I told her. "This guy is really, really funny …"

"Still no."

"Aw, come on … I'll be lonely in the library without you."

Cat paused, taking a long sip of her juice. "Well, then you'll know how I'll feel at the musical auditions this afternoon, and all those rehearsals, too."

There was no point arguing with her. She could be so unreasonable sometimes. I thought about what Gina had said the day before, about Cat putting herself under pressure for the audition. Maybe I wasn't totally to blame for her foul mood. Maybe she was just taking her stress out on me.

Eventually I said, "Did you get Chris's text last night?"

Cat pulled her phone out of her pocket. When the photo and message appeared on the screen, she smiled thinly, clearly pretending she hadn't already seen it.

"Maybe Chris will go to the library and read poetry with you," she quipped.

"Okay," I said, trying to go along with her joke. "I'll ask him." Then I said, "If you're not coming to the library, then I won't go."

Cat shrugged quickly. "No, you should go."

"Nah, I'll hang with you."

"Actually," Cat said breezily, "I was planning to meet Ollie and Paul. We're going to have a jam session. You know, warm up for the audition."

"Who's Paul?" I asked, trying not to frown.

"He's Mrs. Carey's son." Mrs. Carey was our head of music. "He's doing the sound production and lighting for the musical."

"Oh. When did you meet him?"

"Yesterday, while you were in the library. I bumped into Ollie in the hall and he introduced us."

"Oh." *So I'm not the only one keeping significant boy events to themselves*, I thought grimly. I felt slightly betrayed – which made me feel even more guilty for keeping not only the Tony thing to myself, but James, too. But if I brought it up now it would seem a bit pathetic.

"Okay," I said, trying not to sound upset. "Well, I guess I'll see you later then, in English."

"Sure."

I went to the library by myself and sat down with the Catullus anthology. But the words just swam before my eyes. I couldn't concentrate, not with the sick feeling twisting my stomach. I was definitely nervous about the extension class that afternoon, but it was much more than that. My best friend was giving me the cold shoulder, and as far as I was concerned, there was no blacker feeling.

I kept playing my last conversation with Cat over and over in my head. I thought about what would happen if she stopped speaking to me altogether. *What if we never walk each other home again? What if we're not friends anymore?* My heart raced wildly as I considered the worst possible scenarios. I slammed the book shut, breathing hard. I didn't want to do the musical – I wanted to learn Latin. But how was I going to patch things up with Cat?

The final class of the day was English. Our teacher was Miss Lindsay, who Cat and I usually drove crazy with our chatter. This afternoon, we were so quiet that a few minutes into the class Miss Lindsay turned to Cat and asked, "Did you get shot with a tranquilizer dart?"

The entire class erupted into laughter. Cat and I didn't even look at each other.

"Don't you want us to listen, Miss Lindsay?" cooed Cat.

There were more laughs, but I just blushed and looked down at the desk.

We were studying *Jane Eyre* for English, and during class that day we got to watch part of the film version. I kept watching Cat out of the corner of my eye, half expecting her to turn to me and say something funny like, "Ooh, look at Mr. Rochester's unibrow! It's got a life of its own." But her eyes remained glued to the screen.

I so wanted – *needed* – to gossip with her about James. I wanted to analyze yesterday's scene in the library. Did he like me or not? Why had he pulled my hair? Had he done it because he liked me and was trying to get my attention? I could really have used some help sorting out the whole thing. Cat was so good at reading into what people did and said, but I wasn't. Without Cat to help me, I felt clueless.

Towards the end of English, I leaned over to Cat and whispered, "I met a guy in the library yesterday."

Cat remained in profile, her only reaction a slight twitch of her eyebrow.

I continued, trying to make my voice as low and intriguing as possible. "James Whisker. He's in grade 10. He told me that Mrs. Hawkins is always talking about me in his Latin class. Can you believe it?"

"Of course, I'm sure you're always the hottest topic of conversation, Ally," Cat replied at a normal volume, drawing glances from those around us.

"Oh no, I didn't mean it like that," I whispered back. "It just freaked me out … that's all."

In a flash, all kinds of doubts sprang into my mind, mostly about the Latin extension class. What if everyone has already made up their minds about me? What if I can't make friends? What if James has already told everyone how stupid I am? I could imagine everyone talking about me. The thought made me feel sick.

I was afraid of Cat's reply, so I didn't say anything else. I realized how insecure I was without her attention and approval. I felt so wound up about everything that I actually got a fright when the final bell rang.

Cat picked up her bag and took off with a quick wave.

"Hey, Cat!" I called after her. "Good luck! I'll swing by the auditorium after Latin and hopefully I'll get to …" I trailed off as she bounded out of view.

Feeling empty and tired, I packed my bag and headed for Mrs. Hawkins's classroom – slowly, so I wouldn't be the first to arrive.

By the time I got there, the room was full of people, all talking to each other. No one seemed to notice me hovering in the doorway. This was a good sign. I looked around the room and then my stomach flipped. James was sitting at the back, having an animated conversation with the boy next to him. There was a spare seat on his other side. *What would happen if I sat next to him? I* wondered. *Would he remember me?* Of course he would! I was the famous – perhaps even infamous – Ally Motbey. But would he want me to sit next to him? That was another question altogether.

It had been a long time since I'd had to make a friend. I felt out of my depth, especially because there was a boy involved, and a cute, crush-worthy one at that. It was one thing making a fool of myself with him in the library with no one looking on, but now there were lots of people around. People who thought I was a teacher's pet and who probably wanted to see me fall flat on my face. Maybe it would be easier if I just sat by myself.

The other thing was that there was no chair at the empty desk next to James. If I was going to take the plunge and sit next to him, I would have to carry a chair to the back of the room. I scanned the room for spares.

While I was looking around, I noticed a thin-faced, dark-haired girl in the front row trying to catch my eye.

"Ally?" she asked, when I met her gaze.

"Yeah."

The girl smiled warmly. "Thought so." She exchanged a knowing look with the girl sitting next to her. "I'm Ruth and this is Margaret." She gestured to the red-haired girl beside her. "We've heard a lot about you from Mrs. Hawkins."

"Yes, your reputation precedes you," added the redhead Margaret, in a fake snooty voice.

"Oh!" I squeaked. I could feel my cheeks getting hot. I didn't want to be known as the grade 9 Latin try-hard.

I wanted these girls to like me. It would be great to make some new friends. Especially with Cat's mood swinging like a trapeze – it seemed wise to have some backup friends.

"Don't worry," Ruth reassured me. "You're all good." Then she narrowed her eyes, still smiling. "A little *too* good."

I covered my blushing face with my hands.

"Speaking of too good …" continued Ruth, a look of anticipation on her face.

For a brief but terrible moment, I thought there might be a practical joke coming my way. But when I lowered my hands, I saw that Margaret was retrieving a Tupperware container from her bag. Inside the container were lots of tiny cupcakes with white frosting and tiny nuts on top.

"Do you want one, Ally?" asked Margaret.

"Yum!" I exclaimed, clapping my hands together. "What kind are they?"

"Carrot with cream cheese frosting," she said proudly. "And chopped walnuts sprinkled on top."

I picked one out and took a bite. "Oh wow! Double yum!" I wasn't exaggerating. It was absolutely delicious.

"Pretty darn good," agreed Ruth, taking one as well. "You've outdone yourself, Margaret."

Margaret plucked a cupcake out for herself then put the container back in her bag. "I made them during home economics," she said.

"That's the best cupcake I've ever tasted," I said, wiping cake crumbs from the corners of my mouth. "How did you get the frosting so fluffy?"

"I whipped it," explained Margaret, beaming. "You just need to get a bit of air into it."

Our conversation was flowing fast and easy. *These girls are so nice!* I thought. Maybe making new friends wasn't going to be hard after all. I could feel myself beginning to relax.

"Why don't you sit with us, Ally?" asked Margaret. There was a spare desk next to her.

I was just about to sit down when a familiar male voice boomed from the back of the room. "I can smell cake!"

The three of us turned around. Grinning back at us

cheekily was none other than James Whisker.

"I'm sorry," said Margaret with mock seriousness, "but it's all gone."

"Come on, Margaret," pleaded James. "You know how much I love your cakes."

"I know," replied Margaret, shrugging, "but when it's gone, it's gone."

James sighed. He looked supercute, but I didn't want to get caught staring, so I turned back around to face the front.

"That's James Whisker," explained Ruth in a hushed voice. "He lives on my street and he *adores* Margaret's baking. Once he came around to watch a movie and he ate a *whole tray* of her brownies."

"They were particularly great brownies, though," added Margaret.

I didn't mention that I'd already met James. And I certainly didn't say that I'd been thinking about him ever since that meeting. I found myself wishing that James lived on my street, instead of Tony Rickson. I tried to imagine what it would be like having a hot grade 10 guy just over the fence.

"Hey, Ally," said Ruth. "Sit down. Are you waiting for a written invitation?"

"Um …"

Sitting with the girls was definitely a safer, and more subtle, option than lugging a chair to the back of the room just to sit next to James. Who knew what James might say or do if I plonked myself beside him? And anyway, how could I turn down Margaret and Ruth after they'd been so nice to me? And after I'd just scoffed one of Margaret's cupcakes? What was I going to say … *"Er, thanks for the snack, but I'm farsighted and I won't be able to see the whiteboard from the front of the classroom?"*

On the other hand, how great would it be to sit next to James for the whole class? I'd get to exist in that same bubble of nervous excitement I'd floated in yesterday at the library. And maybe – just maybe – I'd find out that my growing crush was mutual. After the whole thing with Tony, where nothing ever got resolved because we were both too shy to say anything, I wanted to actually talk to James.

So where was I going to sit? With the cute boy at the back, or the nice girls up front?

If you think Ally should sit next to James, go to page 148.

If you think Ally should sit with the girls, go to page 169.

Ally ACCEPTS Tony's offer

Chapter Six

I checked myself in the mirror one last time. I was wearing my favorite skinny jeans with an oversized tank top and my new Aztec-print Converse. Cat said it was an outfit I rocked because I was built like a beanpole. Pulling my shoulders back, I smiled casually at my reflection. A maniacally grinning weirdo looked back at me.

I glanced up at Chris. "Okay," I said. "No casual smiles. I'll be cool."

I passed by the kitchen, where my parents were still cleaning up after dinner.

"You look nice, Ally," said Mum. "Are you going somewhere?"

"I'm just going next door," I said, pointing in the direction of the Ricksons' house.

"Next door?" asked Dad, frowning at me over his glasses.

"Tony's helping me prepare for my audition for the school musical. We're just going over one song."

It looked like Dad was trying to suppress a smile. "You're auditioning for a musical? I hope Tony's got his earplugs ready."

I rolled my eyes. "Thanks a lot, Dad."

Mum gave Dad a sharp look. But when she saw me watching her she smiled quickly. "Good for you for giving it a try," said Mum. "Say hi to Sue when you're over there. And be nice to that boy." She stared at me pointedly.

I frowned, wondering what Mum was thinking. "I will," I muttered.

"Be back here by nine."

"Yes, Mum."

I took off before they got another chance to make fun of me. Sometimes I couldn't stand the way my parents knew so much about me – or thought they did. *What a gross invasion of my privacy.*

When I got to the Ricksons' door, my stomach was in knots. Tony opened the door. He'd changed too. Now he was wearing black skinny jeans and a long-sleeved shirt. He looked good, and actually kind of cool. His hair was loose and damp, like he'd just had a shower.

"Hey, come in."

I stepped into the house and looked into the family room. Mrs. Rickson was watching TV and ironing at the same time. It looked like a dangerous pastime to me.

As I walked past, her eyes flicked briefly towards me, and then she turned right around like she was doing a double take. She grinned and waved to me with the hot iron. "Hi, Ally."

Definitely dangerous! "Hi, Mrs. Rickson," I called.

"Can I get you a drink?" offered Tony. "Juice?"

"Um, no thanks," I said.

Tony seemed even more nervous than I was. "Right, then," he said, clapping his hands together. "We might as well get started. My keyboard's in my room."

I followed Tony to his room, which was small and cluttered. In the corner was a desk, crammed with textbooks, a laptop and heaps of sheet music. There were a few posters stuck to the walls, including a signed, framed one of The Beatles. I remembered that from the last time I was here.

It was strange being back in his house. Funny how a place you hadn't been to in a while could dredge up old feelings. Funnier still were the new feelings. There was something weird about being in his bedroom now, especially after our kiss. I wondered whether Tony felt the same way.

I sat on the chair by the desk. Tony knelt by his bed and pulled an electric keyboard out from underneath it. Then he sat on the end of the bed, resting the keyboard on his lap.

"So … where do we start?" I asked nervously.

Tony switched on the keyboard and played a few notes. Then he pressed a button, which started a regular drumbeat. He sped up the beat and turned up the volume.

"I can't believe you wrote all the music for the

whole musical," I blurted out, staring at all the sheet music on his desk.

"Neither can I," he said with a sheepish smile.

"Were you channeling *them*?" I asked, pointing to his Beatles poster.

"I wish. It's not *that* good." Tony put both hands to the keyboard and played some chords in time with the beat. He didn't even look down at his fingers when he played. Still repeating the chords, he said, "So this song is called *Thumbs-up for the Spaniard*. It's supposed to be a kind of anthem. Know what I mean?"

I nodded, but I wasn't certain. "I think so. Like the national anthem?"

Tony looked amused. "Well, sort of. Anyway, the chorus goes:

Thumbs-up, thumbs-up, thumbs-up,
For the Spaniard.
Raise your shield, plunge your sword,
Show your face, Spaniard."

His voice was good – not great – but the song was beyond impressive. The verses were teasing and then the chorus hit an amazing crescendo. And I really got what he meant by an anthem – it was like a call to arms. I loved it. He sang the chorus a few times – and the third time, I surprised myself by joining in.

When I started singing he looked at me and nodded, raising his eyebrows approvingly.

"That was pretty good," said Tony, his deft fingers finally coming to rest. "You *can* sing. It's just a little flat. What you need to do is aim for the note *above* the one you want to sing."

"Okay, I'll try," I said, my face feeling flushed with embarrassment.

"Without me this time."

"Hmm …"

"Come on, I'll play just the melody for you. That way you won't have any trouble picking it up from the chords. Okay … first note." He played a single note and looked to me expectantly.

I opened my mouth, but my throat jammed up. I just squawked – and it definitely wasn't in tune. It was mortifying.

"Cup of hot chocolate?" As if on cue, Mrs. Rickson suddenly appeared at the door. She was holding two steaming mugs.

"Yes, please," I said eagerly.

Mrs. Rickson shuffled over and placed a mug on the desk in front of me.

Tony shook his shaggy head.

"I'll drink it myself, then," chirped his mother, heading for the door. "If you need anything let me know."

"Sorry about that," whispered Tony, when she was gone.

I raised the mug to my lips. "About what?"

"Oh, you know." He shrugged. "Mum. She's all excited about you being here."

I sipped my drink and our eyes met through the steam. He had long, thick eyelashes. We chuckled awkwardly and then both looked away.

"Maybe the hot chocolate will coat my vocal cords and make me sing well."

"It won't," said Tony. "The milk makes you produce phlegm."

"Oh," I said, feeling crestfallen. "Gross."

"It's a fact."

I put the mug back on the desk. "Now I don't feel like it."

Tony looked down at his keyboard, running his fingers absentmindedly over the keys.

I felt so awkward. It was like we were never going to talk about anything serious. I couldn't bear the silence, so I said, "Well, let's give it another try."

"The song?"

"Yeah. Go on. Play it through once without me first though, and then I'll start."

Tony punched out the melody, one key at a time. On the second round I sang, *"Thumbs-up, thumbs-up, thumbs-up for the Spaniard ..."*

After I'd finished the chorus, I faded out to silence.

Tony smiled. "Were you aiming for the note above the one you were trying to sing?"

"No, I forgot! Sorry."

"That was still better, though. That was probably the best singing you've done tonight, actually."

"Let's do it again!" I said, encouraged by his praise.

Tony played it again and this time I tried to aim higher. I hit a few wrong notes, but overall I thought my voice was blending in with the sound of the keyboard, instead of clashing horribly. We went over the chorus a few more times and then Tony played the whole piece properly, with the backup percussion playing. He sang the verses with me, and then he let me pick up the melody of the chorus by myself.

I couldn't believe I was actually singing!

At the end, Tony switched off his keyboard with an exaggerated flourish. He looked pleased. "Not bad, Ally. Not bad at all."

"That felt amazing!" I said, my feet dancing on the spot even though I was sitting down. I knew I was overreacting, but I couldn't help it – I was excited.

Tony, seeming excited too, slapped me a high five before saying, "You've come a long way, but you still need to practice a bit more."

"No!" I pretended to be offended.

He nodded, grinning.

"Ha!" I reached for the mug and took a hearty swig of my not-so-hot chocolate. "Now I can phlegm it up to my heart's content."

Tony laughed. Then he asked, "Do you want to do another session tomorrow?"

"Sure." I drank the rest of my hot chocolate, wondering whether we'd ever discuss the ugly subject of our broken friendship. *Or is it mended now?* I wondered. Just thinking about it made my cheeks hot.

It must have been on Tony's mind too because he blurted out, "I'm really sorry about ... you know ... in the park that time." He trailed off.

I looked at my feet and squirmed. I'd been waiting for so long for Tony to explain himself. If he faltered now, I wasn't sure I'd give him any more chances.

It was so quiet in his room that I could hear the clock ticking on his wall. I waited for ten ticks before standing up.

"I should go," I said, starting for the door.

But just as I did so, Tony opened his mouth. "Hey, Ally, can you close the door?" he asked.

"What?"

"Do you mind closing the door a sec? I just want to talk to you in private."

I thought about just leaving – I really did – but something held me back. I pushed the door gently shut. Then I turned to face Tony.

He was still sitting on his bed with the keyboard in his lap. Still not saying anything. I was getting more annoyed by the second.

Why does he have to be so frustrating? I decided to let him have it. *Really* let him have it. "You led me on last year," I said. "You embarrassed me. And then you never spoke to me again."

I watched him swallow and then fumble for words. "I … I wasn't leading you on, Ally. I just didn't know what to do. I'd wanted to kiss you for ages, but I didn't know how, or if you wanted me to."

Tony's words almost stunned me into silence. Almost. I knew I had to get to the bottom of this, and right now. "Then why didn't you say something?" I demanded, sounding angrier than I felt.

He shook his head. "I don't know exactly. I was nervous. You made me feel … pathetic."

"What do you mean? That's ridiculous. *You* rejected *me!*" I was standing over him now, with my arms folded. I looked away.

"I guess I was surprised. I wasn't expecting *you* to make the move," said Tony. "I'm really sorry. I'm an idiot. A total loser."

"But then you totally ignored me."

Tony paused. He dropped his head and looked down at the keyboard on his lap. "I didn't know what else to do. What can I do to make it up to you?"

I shrugged. "Well, at least you've apologized. Now let's never talk about it again."

Tony raised his head again. He smoothed his hair back with his hands then he lifted up the keyboard and slipped it under his bed. "What if I *want* to talk about it?"

He stood up and, before I knew it, his lips were on mine. He moved his mouth with deliberate slowness for a few seconds before breaking away smoothly.

I literally felt weak at the knees.

We'd only just moved apart when a loud knock sounded at the door. We both jumped. A millisecond later, the door flung open.

"Mu-um!" said Tony.

"Hi, Mrs. Rickson," I said, straightening my tank top and plastering on a wholesome smile. "That hot chocolate was delish!"

"This door should stay open, Tony," she said with an amused, knowing look.

I felt my cheeks getting red, so I looked intently at my watch. "Ooh! I'd better get home." I quickly sneaked by Mrs. Rickson.

"Say hi to your mum for me, Ally," she called after me.

Briefly I turned and waved back over my shoulder. "See ya, Tony. Thanks for the singing lesson."

"See you tomorrow, Ally," said Tony.

"I'll let myself out," I called back to Mrs. Rickson. I could hear her following me up the hallway, but I really didn't want to be around her straight after kissing her son. I was feeling slightly breathless. I could still feel Tony's lips on mine and a dozen thoughts were whirling through my mind.

I dashed out of the Ricksons' house and then skipped all the way to mine, letting myself in quietly – or so I thought.

"It's nearly nine o'clock," said Dad, stepping out of the family room. He was wearing his brightly colored, loud-patterned PJs. He liked them because they were such a contrast to the suit he had to put on every day for work. Sometimes he put them on as soon as he came home.

"I know, I know," I said flippantly.

"You have quite the social life," Dad went on, following me along the hall to my bedroom. "Cat called, by the way. I told her you were next door."

Great, I thought. *So Cat already knows I was at Tony's.*

"I'll call her back," I said, trying not to sound ruffled.

"So is there any glass left in the Ricksons' windowpanes?"

I turned around and rolled my eyes at Dad. He could

be such a stirrer. But then again, so could I.

"Elton John called while you were at work today," I said with a smirk. "He wants his stage costume back. I told him you were wearing it to bed every night. He said to send him a photo."

"Oh, *guffaw, guffaw*," said Dad sarcastically, but I knew I'd won this round. He headed back down the hallway, shaking his head.

Back in my room, my phone was flashing with notifications. There were seven messages and three missed calls. Obviously, Cat had finally resorted to calling my home phone before sending the last text, which read:

R u seriously at Tony's? Call me NOW!

My chest became heavy with dread, and my mind raced with potential explanations. I'd deliberately left my phone at home so I wouldn't have to explain myself if Cat called me and heard Tony in the background. Now I had some serious 'fessing up to do. Or some fast talking. The last thing I wanted was for Cat to start asking Tony questions. What if she zeroed in on him the way she did with Stephen Brent at the dance last year? Tony might never speak to me again. After what had happened tonight, that would be unbearable. I decided to think about it in the morning. I changed into my nightie and got into bed.

Getting to sleep proved more difficult than I had expected. I was still wired from locking lips with Tony. I kept playing the kiss over and over in my mind, and every time I did, my tummy did somersaults and my heart galloped to bursting point in my chest. Why had no one ever warned me about this? Not even Cat, the self-proclaimed world number-one authority on kissing, had been able to explain exactly how it felt. Now I knew … but how could I tell Cat?

Chapter Seven

There was no escape on the bus the next morning. I held my breath as I watched Cat walk down the aisle and drop onto the seat beside me. I knew I was going to have to spill the beans – or at least some of them.

She was wearing a smile, but there was a hardness behind it that I recognized and didn't like.

"So what gives, Motbey?" she asked. "Why were you at Tony's house? And why didn't you answer my texts?"

I took a deep breath, but tried to sound casual. "He was coaching me."

"Coaching you?" She looked genuinely confused. "For what?"

"Singing."

"Oh." This seemed to satisfy her, but only for a moment. She looked at me suspiciously, still smiling. "When was all this arranged?"

Here we go again, I thought, remembering how she'd acted when I told her about hanging out with Tony last year. Cat always had to be in on *everything*. It was almost as if she was scared to lose me, like if she took her eye off me, I might shoot off and never come back.

"It wasn't arranged," I said. "It was last-minute. I just bumped into him on the street on the way home last night and he offered to help me."

"And you *accepted*?" she asked. Her smile was gone.

"Well," I said, trying to sound light. "It's not like I don't *need* help, Cat."

"But I've been helping you," she shot back. Cat folded her arms and looked out the window. After an uncomfortable pause, she turned back to me and said, "You should have told me."

"I'm telling you now."

"Is there something going on with him?"

Is there? I thought. Butterflies gathered in my stomach as my mind turned to the kiss last night. *Well — yes.* But I didn't want to tell Cat. Plus, I was worried about what might happen — or, worse still, *not* happen — with Tony today. He'd been so nice to me last night, but maybe he would ignore me today. My excitement was laced with dread.

I turned to face Cat, trying to look neutral. "There's nothing," I lied.

Cat blinked. Then she grinned, visibly relaxing. "Though he is kind of cute," she said casually.

What does that mean? I thought to myself. The butterflies were still going crazy in my stomach, but I just shrugged. "You go out with him then," I said.

Of course I'd be totally devastated if she went on a date with Tony, but I really wanted to throw her off the scent — at least until I knew what was going on between Tony and me. When I knew for sure something was going on, I'd tell her, I decided.

"Don't be stupid. He's totally your type, Ally. Haven't you noticed?" she went on, her weird intense mood

completely gone. "But I can still say he's pretty hunky …
and those eyes! They're broody, don't you think? Like
there's a lot going on behind them."

I was secretly relieved she wasn't interested in him.
"I haven't really noticed," I replied, betraying nothing.

Sometimes I didn't understand Cat at all.

The first class of the day was English. Tony was also in
our class. When Cat and I walked in, I saw him sitting
in the second row, talking to one of his friends over
the back of his seat. He looked up as we walked past.
Although I'd resolved to ignore him until he'd paid
some serious attention to me, I broke into a shy smile
the moment our eyes met. I couldn't say anything,
though, so I just kept following Cat to the back row.

Once we'd sat down, Cat must have spotted him
because she elbowed me and nodded in his direction.
Then she leaned in and whispered, "Are you telling me
you didn't think Tony's becoming a bit of a hottie?"

I shrugged again.

Cat continued. "I mean, I'm not saying he's in Ollie's league, of course, but —"

I never found out what Cat was going to say because at that moment a whiteboard eraser whistled past her head. Dumbstruck, we looked up to the front of the classroom, where our English teacher, Miss Lindsay, was scowling at us. *When did she arrive?* I wondered.

"I'm glad I've finally got your attention, Caterina. I'm so sorry to interrupt your important chat, but class has started." She was so sarcastic! "Perhaps you'd like to share your opinions with the rest of the class. I presume they have something to do with *Jane Eyre*, given that we're studying it this term. Am I right?"

Even though Miss Lindsay was talking directly to Cat, I felt like I should be in trouble, too. Cat and I glanced at each other, panic-eyed.

"Um …" Cat was speechless.

Miss Lindsay's lips spread in a mean smile. She had a lipstick smear on her front teeth. "Caterina, don't tell me I'm going to have to move you away from Ally again.

You need to stop being so disruptive."

"*No!*" Cat and I cried in unison. Miss Lindsay had separated us for two weeks at the beginning of the year. It had been the bleakest fortnight of my life.

"Then tell me you were discussing the text and not gasbagging about irrelevancies."

I don't know if it was the word "gasbagging" or the lipstick on Miss Lindsay's teeth or my nervous butterfly energy that did it — maybe it was all these things — but suddenly I did a very non-Ally Motbey thing. I burst out laughing — at a teacher. For a few seconds I giggled hysterically. I tried clamping my mouth shut, desperate to stop, but the laugh had to get out somehow. Its chosen route: my nose. To my complete embarrassment, I started honking like a goose. Everyone, including Tony, turned in their chairs to watch the spectacle.

"Alexandra Motbey!" snapped Miss Lindsay. "I expected more from you. Take your things immediately and move to —"

Cat jumped in and cut her off. "Please, Miss Lindsay. We were discussing the text."

Miss Lindsay's eyes narrowed. "Oh really?"

Cat and I both nodded.

"And which particular part of it were you referring to?"

Cat proved a quicker thinker than me. "We were talking about the misunderstandings between Jane and Mr. Rochester that contribute to the, er, the *tension* between them."

"I see," said Miss Lindsay, looking less triumphant than she had a few seconds earlier. "Which misunderstandings are you referring to specifically?"

Cat shook her head thoughtfully. "There are just so many of them. I don't think I could put my finger on anything specific."

Then Tony put his hand in the air.

Miss Lindsay raised her eyebrows in acknowledgement. "Yes, Tony."

He hesitated for a moment, glancing from Miss Lindsay to me and then back again. "Well, I think Jane totally misunderstands Mr. Rochester at first. Because of her past experiences, she thinks the worst of him.

She thinks he's snubbing her when the truth is that he's just too scared tell her how he feels."

I only just stopped myself from gasping. *Is Tony really talking about Mr. Rochester and Jane, or is he talking about him and me?* I wondered. *How totally romantic!* I took a couple of deep breaths and tried to play it cool.

"Tony, that's very insightful," said Miss Lindsay. She looked at me and Cat again and pointed her finger at us. "No more private discussions during class."

"Yes, Miss Lindsay," we said together.

I smiled to myself, feeling sure that Tony's comment about Mr. Rochester and Jane had really been about him and me. I had calmed down by now and knew that I could get through the rest of the class without talking. But I had doubts about Cat. She was still wriggling in her seat as though she had a bunch of fire ants in her undies. I tried to ignore her as she fidgeted and wriggled and tried to catch my eye, until finally she scrawled something on the corner of her notepad and pushed it towards me.

Do you think you could get Tony to set us up on a double date with him and Ollie?

No way! was my gut reaction. I shook my head at Cat.

"Aw, come on, Ally …" She looked at me pleadingly, her hands clasped together. "Please?"

Miss Lindsay heard her and pounced. "Cat, you've used up all nine lives," she said. Everyone laughed, except Cat and me. "Move up front next to –" Miss Lindsay scanned the room for a spare desk "– here, next to Tony."

Grumbling under her breath, Cat picked up her books and went to sit in the second row, right next to Tony.

My stomach twisted. *What was she going to say to him?*

Miss Lindsay glowered at me, then Cat. "Ally, Cat, I want you on opposite sides of the classroom for the next two weeks."

I sighed. Even though Cat could be distracting sometimes, English was so much more fun with her by my side. I slumped back in my chair and watched her and Tony. She wasn't pestering him yet, but it was only a matter of time. She was always so gutsy. I just hoped that she'd keep her mouth shut.

When the bell finally rang, I got up and walked

quickly to the front of the classroom. The butterflies in my stomach were going crazy at the thought of saying hi to Tony. But before I could even do that, Cat was up and standing between us.

"So, Tony reckons that Ollie would be totally into a get-together," said Cat exultantly.

I shot a look at Tony, who was grinning sheepishly. "Hey," he said quietly.

"Hi," I replied shyly. We looked at each other briefly and then looked away, both of us blushing. I could tell he hadn't told Cat anything.

"So, what do you think?" Cat asked me impatiently, apparently not noticing anything out of the ordinary.

I wondered how much pressure Cat had put on Tony, and whether he even wanted to go on a date with me at all. "I'll talk to Ollie," he said. "We could even hang out this afternoon if you're free."

"Yep, we're free," said Cat.

I opened my mouth to protest, but Cat just clapped her hands gleefully.

Tony, who seemed uncomfortable but had obviously

been railroaded into the whole thing, cleared his throat. "Well, what do you guys want to do?"

My mind went into a blank panic. Cat's didn't, though. "Let's go to that café on Green Street."

"No," I said quickly.

"Aw, come on, Ally," said Cat. "It's a really cool café."

"But I don't drink coffee," I said quickly.

Then Tony caught my eye and asked, "What do you want to do, Ally?"

It was a question I rarely heard, and certainly never from Cat. The truth was, I didn't want to go on a double date with Cat and Ollie at all. The stuff between Tony and me was awkward. The fact that I had been hiding it from Cat was even more awkward. The potential for disaster was huge. But Cat was an unstoppable force. To resist her, I would have to become an immovable object.

"I don't want to go to a café," I said, doing my best to be immovable.

Tony shrugged and flashed me a small smile. I guessed he didn't really want to sit at a little table on Green Street having awkward conversations any more

than I did. "Well, maybe you two can talk about it ...
I have to get to history now."

"We'll let you know," said Cat, winking at Tony, as if
to imply the two of them knew better than me.

As soon as Tony left, Cat began to berate me. "What
were you *thinking*?" she hissed.

But my attention was on Tony. At the door, he
stopped and glanced meaningfully over his shoulder at
me. I smiled at him and he left the classroom with a
little wave.

Cat hadn't stopped talking "... only chance to get
Ollie's attention. Ally, are you even *listening*?"

I blinked at Cat, who was gesturing wildly at me.

"Sorry?"

"Ally!"

"Sorry, I —"

"What's wrong with you today?"

"Nothing." I took a deep breath and tried to sound
calm. "Really. I just don't want to go to a café with those
guys. It'll be super awkward."

"But you and Tony are all hunky-dory buddies now,

right?" Then she added cattily, "Now that he's been teaching you to sing."

I shrugged, trying to think of something to say.

But Cat wasn't finished. "And what's your problem with the café, anyway? I mean, that's what people do on dates ... go to cafés or restaurants. What do you want to do, Ally? Go to the playground at the park or something lame like that?"

Cat was being really awful. Was it just because I didn't want to go to the café with the boys? Or was it that she could tell I was keeping something big from her? I felt a strong urge to just agree to the double date. Maybe the four of us *could* go somewhere together. Maybe it could be okay.

"Anyway," Cat said, zipping up her pencil case with finality. "I've got Italian." Without making eye contact with me, she picked up her books and marched out of the classroom.

My stomach lurched. "See you at recess!" I called out after her. I looked down at my hands as I packed up my stuff, and saw they were shaking. Were Cat and I having a fight?

I made my way to French, my mind whirring, my insides coiled like a spring. I couldn't believe that Cat was being so horrible to me. Especially when I'd given up the Latin extension class to do the musical with her and everything. We were supposed to be besties, but it was like she didn't even care that I was totally stressing out.

Suddenly it occurred to me that Cat couldn't know that she was putting me under stress ... she didn't know about Tony and me and the kiss. And I hadn't told her about last year. So how could she know that a double date would be torture? She didn't know about the secret that was gnawing inside me.

Suddenly I wondered if maybe *I* was the one being unfair. Cat was pushy and nosy, but she did always share everything with me. I always knew what she was feeling — it wasn't always nice, but at least I knew where I stood with her. But how could she know what was going on with me if I didn't tell her?

I took a seat at the back of the class, wondering whether it was time to come clean. I had a secret that I'd been keeping for almost a year. Was I brave enough

to reveal it? I knew Cat's reaction was likely to be …
well, explosive. But at least then it would be out in the
open.

On the other hand, couldn't friends – even best
friends – keep some things from each other? Cat and I
were in each other's pockets all the time, finishing each
other's sentences, walking each other home … Wasn't
I entitled to something that was mine and only mine?
Why did Cat have to know *everything*?

I noisily organized my books and pencils on the
desk, then thumped down my French textbook. It was
time to make a decision.

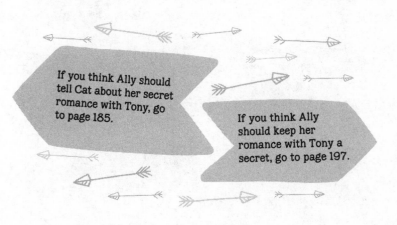

If you think Ally should
tell Cat about her secret
romance with Tony, go
to page 185.

If you think Ally
should keep her
romance with Tony a
secret, go to page 197.

Ally REFUSES Tony's offer

Chapter Six

The final bell rang on Friday afternoon and my stomach clenched.

Cat jumped up from her desk and whooped. "It's time to *get in the arena!*" she shrieked. Since Wednesday, Cat had started calling the auditorium the "arena" in honor of *Gladiator*.

Our English teacher, Miss Lindsay, came over and spoke above the noise of everyone packing up. "I hope you heard the homework I gave, Caterina-Cordelia," she said. "I expect you to have finished *Jane Eyre* by Monday."

But Cat just waved her hand dismissively. "I've watched the movie," she said, "and I've heard the song."

"What song?" asked Miss Lindsay, suspiciously.

"The one by Kate Bush that my mum loves." She cleared her throat and let rip in a high-pitched falsetto: "*I've come …*"

Miss Lindsay rolled her eyes and almost looked amused. "Cat, that song's called *Wuthering Heights*. You've got the wrong book and the wrong Brontë sister. Read *Jane Eyre*, okay? The book by Charlotte Brontë."

"Yes, Miss Lindsay," said Cat, as she tossed her pristine, unopened copy of *Jane Eyre* into her bag.

Cat and I half jogged to the "arena." There were already a few people there, sitting in the back row being cool. We sat right in front, near the stage. Who could think about being cool at a time like this? I just wanted to avoid utter humiliation.

Louisa and her stuck-up posse arrived not long after us and installed themselves up front on the other side of the aisle. Louisa and Cat eyed each other.

With two great singers and only one great female part, this audition was going to be a fight to the death. Louisa seemed nervous. Jiggling her knee up and down, she started humming some scales.

"I hope they let us warm up before they audition us," said Cat. "I don't sing well cold."

"I'm sure they'll let us warm up," I assured her. "But it won't make any difference for me."

Cat giggled. "You'll be okay, Ally."

Tony came scuffing up the aisle and climbed up onto the stage carrying a messy pile of handwritten sheet music. He looked like a disheveled composer – nutty, but also quite cute. I realized I had butterflies in my stomach – and not just because of the audition.

I had avoided him all week and suddenly I felt kind of bad about it. I also wondered what I'd given up by avoiding him. Maybe he could have helped me. Then again, maybe I would have just dug my grave of embarrassment even deeper. One thing was for sure, I felt really good about him offering me help. I had a feeling that things wouldn't be so awkward between us anymore.

Suddenly Tony was looking right at me, as if he could sense me thinking about him. I looked away and sat up very straight in my seat.

Cat noticed. "What's going on?" she asked.

"Nothing," I said lightly, not trusting myself to look her in the eye.

"Are you sure?" she crooned teasingly. "You're not keeping something from me, are you, Ally?"

Cat's teasing was lighthearted, but it was starting to irritate me. And it made me pretty determined not to let on to Cat about Tony, not if she was going to torture me with it like this.

"Yep," I said curtly. "There's nothing to talk about."

"You're being very defensive, Alexandra."

"Just drop it, okay?"

"Why so touchy?"

"Stop it!" I *was* touchy now. "I'm trying to focus on the audition." Then I added pointedly, "The audition I really don't want to do."

Cat scoffed. "Don't be silly. It's going to be so much fun doing the play together."

While we we'd been bickering, the auditorium had filled up a lot. Looking around, I saw that Ollie had arrived, with a group of other grade 10 boys – as well as Paul Carey, who was looking pretty dashing in his Penscombe uniform.

Mrs. Carey and one of the other music teachers were up near the stage, talking to Tony. Mrs. Carey turned to face the audience and clapped her hands to get our attention. The auditorium fell instantly silent.

My palms started sweating. My throat thickened – I felt like I couldn't even speak, let alone sing. It was pathetic how unprepared I was. *Why*, I asked myself as I wiped my sweaty hands along my skirt, *did I not accept Tony Rickson's offer of help with the audition?* I swallowed hard, trying to clear my throat. I could tell that I was about to pay the price for being a wimp.

"We're going to run through one of the songs from this wonderful new musical. It's called *Thumbs-up for the Spaniard*. You're all going to audition with it this afternoon. It's written by Tony Rickson from grade 9, and he's going to accompany us on the piano."

There was a burst of applause and cheering for Tony. I clapped my hands together automatically. My heart was racing in my chest at Olympic speed.

Mrs. Carey waved us silent. "Not that he doesn't deserve it," she said. "But we have a lot of auditions to get through this afternoon. I'll pass out some sheet music and then we're going to sing through the song a couple of times. After that each of you will come up on stage and sing the chorus by yourself."

My nerves and the butterflies in my stomach became full-blown panic. The idea of singing on stage alone had always filled me with terror. Now that I was actually in a room with all the people who were going to see me make a fool of myself, I was mortified on a whole new level. I looked down at the sheet music that Cat had just passed me. The notes and words swam before my eyes. *How do people read music?* I wondered. It just looked like a whole mess of lines and dots.

When Tony played the introduction on the piano, the sheet music made a lot more sense. The notes were strong – catchy even – and when everyone else started singing, I thought, *Well, here goes.* But when I opened my mouth to join in, no sound came out. Not a squeak. My nerves had completely clamped my throat shut.

I mouthed the words, still unable to produce a note. How on earth was I going to stand up on stage and sing on my own? It was impossible.

I felt a huge weight start to press down on me. I had to run. "C-Cat," I stuttered throatily. "I have to go."

Cat turned to me. "What?"

I could hardly breathe. My head was spinning as I looked around at the sea of singing faces. I had to get out of there. And fast.

Without a second glance at my bestie, I turned and ran down the aisle and through the double doors.

Chapter Seven

Leaning against the coolness of the hallway wall with my eyes closed, my breath soon slowed. With every passing second my legs were feeling less jellylike.

With my eyes still closed, I heard the doors of the auditorium open and close again.

"Ally?"

It was Paul Carey.

"Oh, hi." I tried to sound normal. "It's hot in there, isn't it?" I put my hand to my forehead and pretended to swoon.

Paul wasn't fooled. "You're nervous," he said. "It's meant to be fun," he added, taking a step towards me.

Then something weird happened. My eyes filled with tears. I wasn't crying because I was sad or upset. I was crying because he recognized what I was going through. And he didn't try to dismiss it. Not even my best friend had realized how stressed-out I was about the audition, but here was Paul, a guy I'd only met once before, understanding me. He looked so serious and concerned, and it made my heart thump – in appreciation this time, not from nerves.

Before I knew it I was leaning into him. He held me steady, one arm around my shoulders, the other scooping my waist. He was strong and warm. I pressed my face into his wool blazer.

"You don't have to audition, you know."

"Yes, I do."

"But if you don't like singing, you're not going to enjoy it."

I lifted my head to look at him. "That's not the point," I said. "Cat needs me."

I realized I was still wrapped in his arms. I felt slightly awkward, but it was so warm and comfortable that I didn't want to move. Paul's face was just inches from mine. We locked gazes. My stomach dropped. I thought he was going to kiss me … hoped he would, but then …

Suddenly, the auditorium's double doors swung open. "Paul Gregory Carey!" came an outraged hiss.

Paul and I jumped apart.

"Oh … er … hi, Mum." Paul sounded about six years old.

"Hi, *indeed*," spat Mrs. Carey, who was glowering at us with the stormiest expression I'd ever seen. "Get back in here, this minute!"

"Yes, Mum," mumbled Paul. He didn't even look at me before slinking back into the auditorium, his head bowed. He must have been mortified. I felt pretty mortified myself.

Mrs. Carey turned to me, squinting. "What's your name?"

I gulped. Mrs. Carey was fearsome enough when she *hadn't* just caught you embracing her son. My answer was a squeak. "Um … Ally Motbey."

"Are you auditioning for the musical, Ally?"

Could I go back into the auditorium after what had just happened? I imagined standing onstage – alone – and singing out of tune in front of all those people. This awful thought sealed my answer. "No," I said firmly.

"What are you doing here then?"

"Um … I left my bag in the auditorium."

Mrs. Carey rolled her eyes. "Go and get it, then."

I walked past her, through the doors and into the aisle of the auditorium. Louisa Andrews was on the stage, obviously waiting for Mrs. Carey to return. She was fiddling with the pleats of her skirt. I moved quickly up the aisle to where Cat was sitting, arms folded over her chest. It was as if she was defending herself against Louisa.

"Everything okay?" she asked when she saw me.

I shook my head.

"What's wrong?"

I took a deep breath and came clean. "I'm not going to audition, Cat. I don't want to audition and I don't want to be in the musical."

I reached down to retrieve my schoolbag, but Cat stood up, getting in my way so I couldn't reach it. I straightened up again and found myself eye to eye with my best friend.

"I can't believe this, Ally," she said. "What's going on?" Her voice started to rise above the general murmur of the crowd. People turned to look at us.

I felt a surge of anger that surprised me. "Let me get my bag," I said through gritted teeth.

"But you promised!" Cat's tone was both pleading and demanding.

"But I don't want to do the musical!" I shout-whispered. "I *never* wanted to do it! I wanted to go to the Latin extension class, but I sacrificed that for *you*!"

"For *me*?" shrieked Cat. She sneered. "Yeah, tough choice: between a great musical and a Latin class." By now she wasn't even trying to keep her voice down. A hush had fallen over the room and everyone was gawking at us. Cat didn't seem to notice.

"Just let me get my bag – *please*!" I hissed. "I have to leave."

Cat stamped her foot on the floor and kicked at my schoolbag. It was incredible. I'd only seen her act this way once, during a fight with her father when he wouldn't let her go to her cousin's party, which was being held at a bar. On the rare occasions when someone actually stood up to her, Cat really didn't react well.

Then, just when I thought she couldn't make bigger fools of us, she stepped towards me and raised her voice even more. Her eyes were flashing with rage. "Fine!" she shouted. "I thought you were supposed to be my best friend, Ally Motbey. But I don't care – just go home, go to your room, lie on your bed and stare up at your imaginary boyfriend. I'm pretty sure he's the only person in the world who can stand your singing!"

There was a ripple of laughter, then everyone started talking at once, in low voices. Cat's eyes flashed around the auditorium. It was like she had just realized other people were around. While she was distracted, I retrieved my bag.

As I slipped into the aisle, Mrs. Carey came marching up, her long floral skirt swooshing around her legs.

"Enough, Cat," she snapped. Then she glared at me, as if I were the one causing all the trouble. "Good-bye, Amy."

I didn't bother correcting her. I just hurried down the aisle. I kept my eyes downcast, but still absorbed every jeer and smirk around me.

As I approached the doors, I heard Cat say chirpily, "Well, that warmed my voice up. Now I'm really ready to sing!"

This was followed by titters and giggles. I stopped in my tracks and turned around to face the stage.

After all I've done to keep Cat happy, I thought, *now I'm the butt of her joke? What am I? Some kind of doormat?* I felt like Julius Caesar getting knifed by Brutus. It was like something inside me had crossed over. I wasn't sure exactly what it was, but it was white-hot and ugly. A surge of fury filled my chest. I was not going to lie down and die.

Words flooded into my mind and I found I had quite a few things to say to Cat. She wasn't the only one who could make sensitive, personal announcements in public. I wheeled around to let her have it, but something stopped me.

I wasn't high-strung and impulsive like Cat. I was thoughtful and considered, and always agonized about things before I did them. Now I wondered if maybe it was time to ditch cautious, measured Ally, and give Cat a taste of her own medicine. But I didn't hate her. Yes, she had hurt my feelings deeply and I wanted to teach her a lesson. But what if I said something I regretted? What if I ruined our friendship?

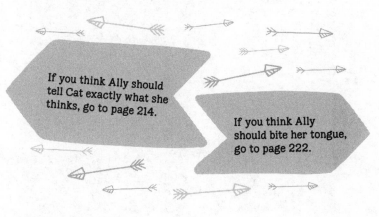

If you think Ally should tell Cat exactly what she thinks, go to page 214.

If you think Ally should bite her tongue, go to page 222.

Ally SITS *next to* James

Chapter Seven

"I'm sorry," I told the girls, grimacing. "I can't sit in the front row. Mrs. Hawkins spits when she says 's.' She read part of *The Aeneid* to us last year and every time she said 'Aeneas,' the people sitting at the front had to close their eyes. It was like it was raining inside."

This was a wild exaggeration. Mrs. Hawkins did have a tiny lisp, but not to the extent of flying spittle. I felt a bit bad when I saw the quizzical glances Ruth and Margaret were exchanging. But I wasn't going to stick around for questions or comments. "Thanks again for the cupcake," I said quickly, as I grabbed the chair from under the desk beside Margaret and headed to the back of the room.

"Hey! Library buddy!" said James. He got up to help me with the chair. "How did you do with the poems?"

"Turned out the anthology's a reference book," I replied. "So I couldn't borrow it."

James chuckled. "Did Mrs. Gray look at you like you were a terrorist when you tried to borrow it?"

"Yeah, how did you know?" I asked.

"Just a suspicion." He leaned back in his chair, smiling. He really was seriously cute. "So you resorted to the Internet?"

I nodded. James's blue eyes sparkled through his glasses.

There was just enough time for him to introduce me to his friend Matthew before Mrs. Hawkins came in. She was carrying a huge stack of stapled paper bundles.

"Good afternoon, *discipuli*," she said, thudding the pile of paper onto her desk.

"Good afternoon, *magistra*," the class replied as one. In the grade 9 Latin class, we still hadn't entered into any of this *discipuli/magistra* stuff, but I was looking forward to it. It was quaint.

"So, this is what the cream of the crop looks like," she said with a smile, sitting on the edge of her desk. "Thank you all for coming to this special class. If you're here it's because you've shown talent for what we're about to do today, which is to construe some difficult Latin poetry."

"Construing" was basically translating, but you had to make the translation sound good in English. It was hard because many Latin words and phrases didn't have a simple English equivalent.

Mrs. Hawkins laid a hand on the stack of papers she had brought in. "I'm going to pass out copies of three poems and a vocab list. Then I'll give you a few minutes to read the poems and translate any unusual words using the vocab list. After that I'm going to ask each of you in turn to construe a line from the poems."

Wow, I thought. *She's really throwing us in at the deep end!* Luckily, I wasn't the only one who thought this was going to be tough. The class was buzzing.

"Piece of cake!" James called out, laughing.

"Now, now," said Mrs. Hawkins, passing the papers out. "Don't worry about making mistakes. This is college-level Latin. I don't expect a perfect interpretation. I just want you to try."

While the photocopied bundles were being handed out, James looked at me with a pained expression. In spite of the look on his face, my heart skipped a beat. "I hope she didn't pick the poem about smelly Rufus," he said.

I giggled, knowing exactly what he was talking about, then looked down at the first page of the handout. I recognized the poem, a love poem to Catullus's girlfriend, Lesbia. It was one of the easier ones: *Lesbia, you ask how many kisses of yours would be enough and more to satisfy me* ... My face flushed, knowing that, right beside me, James was reading these same words. I quickly turned the page.

James leaned across and whispered, "Wow! That was fast. Mrs. Hawkins must be right about you."

I blushed even harder. The next poem was a five-liner. I vaguely remembered it. It mentioned someone called "Furius," which wasn't a name you could easily forget. Furius was yet another Roman who Catullus had it in for. Looking at the poem now, I knew it had something to with Furius being a cheapskate, but I couldn't translate it.

"I'll bet this poem made Furius furious," I whispered to James, trying to make him laugh.

He glanced at me sideways. "Sorry?"

"I said, I'll bet this poem made Furius furious."

James looked confused. Then I realized that he was still reading the first poem and had no idea what I was talking about. My joke had fallen flat. "The poem on the next page," I said.

James put his hands in the air. "Whoa there, genius. I'm still trying to work out how many kisses are enough."

"Sorry …" Now my face was really burning. I decided not to make any further attempts at humor. I turned the page and started reading the third poem, but I wasn't really absorbing any of the words.

Before I knew it, Mrs. Hawkins was telling us to

turn back to the first page.

"Ruth," she said, "could you take us through the first two lines of the poem to Lesbia? First in Latin, then in English. Now remember your Latin pronunciation. Hard c's only, okay?"

Ruth did a great job, and only got one word wrong. There was a short round of clapping when she was done.

"Hold your applause," said Mrs. Hawkins. "We have a lot to get through – your hands will be raw by the end of it."

"Can we heckle?" called James. Everyone cracked up.

Mrs. Hawkins tried not to smile. "No, James. Please don't heckle. This isn't gladiatorial combat. Go to the auditorium for that."

My tummy lurched uncomfortably. The *Gladiator* auditions! I pictured Cat fuming at the back of the auditorium, thinking about what a terrible friend I was. Hoping that I'd be able to catch the end of the audition, I pushed the image out of my mind. It was so complicated. By now she'd probably convinced herself that she didn't even want me there.

We got through the rest of the poem slowly, Mrs. Hawkins picking people at random to construe the lines. I wanted to get lines from the Lesbia poem because I knew what most of it meant, but when we got to the final two lines, she asked James to construe them. Truthfully, he didn't do a great job, construing "nor an evil tongue trick us" as "nor bad language fascinate us." But it was funny, and he didn't seem embarrassed.

Then we started the poem about Furius. It was really hard, and Mrs. Hawkins only asked for one line at a time. I had my fingers crossed she wouldn't ask me. Waiting to find out who was next was like sitting through a game of Russian roulette. When we got to the fifth line, she uttered two terrible words: "Ally Motbey."

I squirmed in my chair and put my pen on the first word. I knew I had read the English translation last night, but with only the Latin in front of me, I just couldn't work out what it said. "Um…" I began.

"Take your time, Ally."

I stared at the line for what seemed like minutes. *Uerum ad milia quindecim et ducentos.* It didn't mean anything to me, except that I was fairly sure the word "*decim*" meant "ten." My mind was slow and murky, the classroom absolutely silent. I wanted to sink into the floor. This was exactly the kind of situation I'd been hoping to avoid. I looked up helplessly at Mrs. Hawkins.

Thankfully she took pity on me and gave me a clue. "Catullus is making fun of Furius because Furius has a mortgage," she said.

"He's accusing Furius of being a cheapskate," I ventured, almost as a question.

"In a way, yes."

Suddenly I remembered what the poem was about, and I gasped. In English it was called *Poverty: To Furius*, and in it Catullus accused Furius of being so stingy and shriveled that he barely did ten poos a year. That was about as sophisticated as Catullus's insults got. *Aha!* I thought. *That's the line.*

"You look like you've had a lightbulb moment," said Mrs. Hawkins.

"Are you sure you want me to construe it?" I asked cautiously. It was a pretty gross poem in my opinion.

"Go ahead, Ally."

And so I read out the line in Latin, and then I said, "… and in English it means, 'you don't even poo ten times a year.'" I had hardly finished speaking when I started to giggle.

In an instant I was joined by the rest of the class. Beside me, James was roaring with laughter. People in the rows in front turned around to gape. Some of them were laughing so hard they had tears in their eyes.

I looked up at Mrs. Hawkins and saw that she was shaking her head, her hand covering a huge grin, and I realized I was being laughed *at*, not *with*. Mrs. Hawkins waited for the laughter to die down before speaking. "Ally, the line you just quoted is from a poem called *Poverty: To Furius*. The poem we're construing today is called *The Mortgage: To Furius*, and the line I asked you to look at refers to the size of Furius's mortgage, not to his toilet habits. It means, 'your house is exposed to a mortgage of fifteen thousand, two hundred.' Maybe spend a little bit more time concentrating on what you're reading, as opposed to relying on your memory."

I dropped my head into my hands as shrieks of laughter rang out all around me. There was no point in trying to pretend I'd deliberately mixed up the poems. It must have been obvious to everyone that I'd been reading English translations on the sly, and now I'd been tripped up in the most embarrassing way. I'd never been so humiliated in my life. Here I was, the much talked about Latin student, outed as a fraud! All I could do was keep my face covered until Mrs. Hawkins, who seemed to be on the edge of giggles herself, moved on to the next poem..

At long last, we finished the third poem and Mrs. Hawkins handed out another bundle of poems for us to read before the next class. I swept the papers straight into my bag and made a beeline for the door, eyes to the floor. After disgracing myself so spectacularly, I couldn't bear to even look at James, who'd laughed the loudest of anyone. As I continued my hasty retreat, my face hot with blushing, I realized that I'd moved from "teacher's pet" to "class joke" in the space of half an hour. I wasn't sure which title was worse.

Longing for someone to unload on, I headed to the auditorium. I hoped I hadn't missed Cat's audition. That really would be a terrible end to an already bad afternoon.

Chapter Eight

Cat was sitting in the second row from the front, next to Ollie Haas. I slipped silently into the empty seat on the other side of her.

The moment she saw me, her green eyes lit up, and in the next few seconds she seemed to make a conscious effort to play it cool. "Well, well, well," she said. "Look who found time to swing by."

"You haven't already had your audition, have you?" I whispered.

Cat gestured to the stage. "I'm next," she said flatly. She wasn't giving me anything for turning up. She didn't even look at me.

But I wasn't ready to give up trying to fix things. "Go for it, Cat!"

My words of encouragement must have been too loud because there were a couple of "shushes" from behind us. I clasped my hands in my lap and focused on the flat, less-than-impressive voice of the girl auditioning. The grade 10 Latin extension class was suddenly a world away.

When Cat's name was called, she wiped her hands on her skirt and shimmied past me into the aisle. That was when I noticed that Tony Rickson was on the stage behind an upright piano. His hair was tied in a neat ponytail and for once he didn't seem to be hiding behind his shaggy mane. I realized that he'd changed a lot since last year. We both had. It was silly to keep dwelling on that lousy kiss as if it was the most important thing in the world. Maybe it was time to let it go.

Anyway, there were more important things at stake. I glanced around, looking for Louisa Andrews. I spotted her, sitting with her legs daintily crossed, just across the aisle. Her eyes were fixed on Cat. She was probably hoping that Cat would make a complete mess of the audition. Turning back to the stage, I crossed my fingers that the opposite would occur. I knew that only a very bad case of nerves could stop Cat from totally killing this audition.

From the piano, Tony mouthed, *Ready?* When Cat nodded, he started hammering the piano keys. I knew Tony had written the song, and I had to admit, it was a very catchy tune. I was impressed. When it was time for Cat to start singing, I noticed that he paused for just a moment and looked over at her expectantly. She didn't need her hand held, though, and she came in at exactly the right time:

"Thumbs-up, thumbs-up, thumbs-up
For the Spaniard ..."

Her voice was as strong and clear as ever, and perfectly in tune. She was so confident that she even used sweeping, dramatic hand gestures as she sang. A few seats away from me, Ollie said something to the guy sitting next to him and they both whooped and held their thumbs-up. By the end of the song, most of the people in the auditorium had their thumbs in the air. I couldn't help stealing a glance at Louisa. She was smirking, but I knew underneath it she must have been feeling rattled. *Good*, I thought.

Cat got a huge round of applause. Some people even giving her a standing ovation. Even the head of music, Mrs. Carey, who was in charge of giving out the parts, had a generous smile on her face. Everyone knew that Mrs. Carey was really tough, so I knew this was a very good sign.

Obviously delighted, Cat strode down the aisle with a flushed face and a big smile. People in the row ahead of me congratulated her and patted her shoulders as she walked by.

I stood and held my arms out to embrace her. "That was amaz–" I stopped mid-word as Cat breezed straight past me and flew into Ollie's arms.

"Amazing!" boomed Ollie, as if he was finishing my sentence.

With a self-conscious glance around me, I turned my unrequited hug into a stretch and sat back down.

I felt like I'd just been slapped in the face. Though I thought it was really cool that Ollie and Cat were growing so close, being completely ignored felt mean. What was Cat's problem? I was here, wasn't I?

I would have walked straight out but I knew Cat wouldn't have followed me, even if she'd noticed me leaving, which seemed unlikely. When she sat down, she had her back to me, and she continued jabbering to Ollie, who was gazing at her adoringly. When she finally turned to face the front, I finished my compliment. "That was great," I whispered.

"How was your Latin class?" she asked with a frown.

"Disaster," I admitted.

Cat seemed a little cheered. "What happened?"

But I didn't get to tell her any more because Mrs. Carey, exasperated by the commotion following Cat's audition, had to get up on stage and yell at everyone to be quiet. The din died down, but no one who sang after Cat was anywhere near as good as her. I felt sorry for every single one of them – except for Louisa Andrews, who auditioned last.

"Oh, here we go," whispered Cat as Louisa strode confidently onto the stage. "Dame Kiri Te Kanawa, eat your heart out."

I scoffed sympathetically, hoping Cat would think that I knew who Dame Kiri what's-her-name was. She knew so much random music stuff.

Louisa's audition was good — *very* good. But she treated the Cherrywood High auditorium like a concert hall, blasting out the song in explosive vibrato. The girl could sing — I couldn't deny that — but even I could tell that her voice wouldn't suit a modern musical. Her friends gave her a standing ovation, but I knew they were just being nice. It was clear who'd be getting the part of Lucilla. Cat had stolen the lead!

Afterwards, I followed Cat to the area just outside the auditorium, where everyone was gathering to chat and panic and dissect the auditions. She didn't wait for me or even look at me. I practically had to chase her out. Her attention was divided between Ollie and a tall boy in a private school uniform who I assumed was Mrs. Carey's son. Cat didn't bother to introduce us.

When they finished discussing the musical, the conversation moved on to a soccer match, which it seemed Cat was invited to.

"When's the match?" I asked hopefully. I tried to look as forlorn as possible, hoping that Cat would take pity on me and invite me.

It didn't happen, though. Cat looked at me coldly, like she really didn't want me to be part of her new social set. She rolled her eyes, then turned her back on me. Then she went right on talking to Ollie and the boy I assumed was Paul, as if I hadn't said a word. She was completely freezing me out!

I was so shocked by her rudeness that I just stood there, my mouth hanging open. Ollie must have taken pity on me because he turned to me and said, "It's tomorrow morning. Down at the field."

Cat shot him a look, as if to say, *Why are you talking to her?*

Then, without even looking at me, she said, "It's for people in the musical, Ally. Not just randoms, okay?"

"Oh."

As a "random," I was clearly not invited.

As the conversation went on without me I felt smaller and smaller, sadder and sadder, until I thought I might actually disappear.

I had to sort things out with Cat or I was going to lose her to the musical and her new friends. The worst thing was that the nicer I was to Cat, the meaner she seemed to act. It was time to put a stop to it, one way or another.

But how? If I forced Cat to explain herself this afternoon, at least the confrontation would be over and done with. Then again, perhaps I'd be doing exactly what she wanted me to do. Maybe she *wanted* to break up our friendship.

Maybe it would be better if I just took off and gave her a taste of her own medicine. I was pretty sure that she'd hate being ignored just as much as I did. And if she really didn't want to be my friend anymore, I guess I'd find out eventually … when she didn't call, or visit, or talk to me ever again.

What was I going to do? Should I storm off with

my Latin homework tucked in my schoolbag, or should I drag Cat aside and have it out with her? Did I really have the guts?

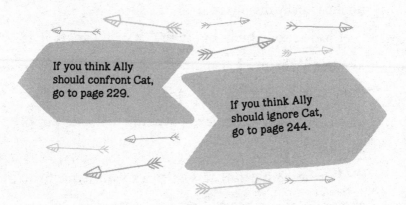

If you think Ally should confront Cat, go to page 229.

If you think Ally should ignore Cat, go to page 244.

Ally SITS *with the girls*

Chapter Seven

"That class was totally exhausting," I said to Ruth and Margaret as Mrs. Hawkins left the room at the end of our first Latin extension class.

"It wasn't that bad," Ruth replied.

"Maybe not for you," I said, glancing appreciatively at Margaret. "But if Margaret hadn't helped me with that line about Furius's mortgage, I would have made a total fool of myself. I feel like I've just been dodging bullets."

Both girls giggled. We'd only known each other for an hour, but it was already like we were old friends. Ruth was soft-spoken and friendly, and Margaret was brassy and raucous. And as well as being really, really cool girls, they were both very smart and I could tell that they were right at the top of their Latin class.

"You know what, Ally?" said Margaret. "No offense, but before today, we thought you'd be a nerd."

"It's just the way Mrs. Hawkins talks about you," added Ruth, in a kind voice. "Like you know absolutely everything about Latin."

"Yeah," said Margaret. "We were expecting a boring know-it-all."

"I'm glad you're giving me a chance," I said. "You guys are way better than me at this stuff. I just wish Mrs. Hawkins hadn't talked me up to everyone. It's *so* embarrassing."

"Hey, at least you have a reputation as a genius," said Ruth. "Could be worse."

I felt a little bit better, and hoped I would soon just become part of the class.

Though I hadn't thought about him much during the lesson – I had been way too busy concentrating on the poems we were construing – James Whisker now drifted into my mind. I could hear him talking to someone behind us, and while I desperately wanted to turn around, I didn't want him to know I was looking. So I used a technique I'd seen Louisa Andrews use to check out Ollie.

I brought my braid over my shoulder and fiddled with the end. Then I flicked my head quickly so the braid went flying back the way it came. As I did this, I looked over my shoulder for the briefest of moments. It was a simple, but crafty move.

Unfortunately, my timing was terrible! In the brief moment I was looking over my shoulder, James was looking right at me. I saw him raise his hand as if to wave, but I had whipped back around to the front before I could see or do anything else, and I didn't dare look back.

"Ally?"

I'd been so distracted by trying to peek at James that I didn't realize Ruth had been talking to me. "Sorry?" I said.

"I asked what you thought of the new poems Mrs. Hawkins gave us for homework."

I groaned. "Impossible!"

"They look diabolical, don't they?" said Margaret, frowning as she looked through the handout Mrs. Hawkins had given us.

"*Diabolus*," I agreed. It was Latin for "devil" and was one of the words on the vocab list Mrs. Hawkins had given us. It was cool to discover the Latin origins of words we use every day.

Margaret laughed as she packed up her books, and turned to Ruth. "So, our first impressions were right. Ally *is* a nerd."

They both giggled, but I knew they were laughing *with* me, not *at* me. It was a relief to find out that not all older girls were as diabolical as Louisa Andrews.

All of a sudden Margaret stopped giggling. I followed her gaze to the object of her panic and then looked quickly away. James had packed up his things and was walking towards the door. When I looked back at Margaret, I saw that her freckly face had turned beet red and she was now looking at the floor.

As James passed us, he paused, as if he wanted to say something, but then he continued out into the hall.

The second he was gone, Ruth burst into laughter.

"Stop it!" whined Margaret. "You're making it worse."

"*What?*" said Ruth in mock innocence. "What did I do? I didn't even *look* at him."

"Look at who?" I asked cautiously.

"James, of course," whispered Ruth, her face lighting up. "Margaret's in love with him."

"I am *not!*"

"She thinks he's *luscious*, don't you, Margaret? You're blushing!"

I tried to ignore the funny feeling in my stomach. *If I like James, and Margaret likes James, this class could get complicated*, I thought.

I wondered whether I should say something about what had happened with James in the library. Would it make Margaret jealous? Maybe it would be better if I just kept quiet.

"What do you think, Ally?" asked Margaret in a secretive tone, her cheeks still red. In the time it had taken James to walk out of the classroom, she'd gone from confident and rowdy to embarrassed and meek.

"He seems nice," I said, deliberately not letting anything on.

"He used to be a skinny little nerd," said Ruth. "Then when we came back to school after Christmas, he'd transformed into a … a …" Her eyes rolled upward as she searched for the right words.

"A skinny, tall hottie?" suggested Margaret with a wide grin.

Ruth wrinkled her nose. "I wouldn't go that far."

"He's just so much cuter now. He's *handsome*. And I like his voice," mooned Margaret, clasping her bag to her chest. "It's so smooth."

Ruth shook her head and gave me a conspiratorial look. "Can you believe this girl?"

I shrugged, my stomach still turning. "I kind of get where Margaret's coming from."

"Watch out," said Ruth, teasing. "I don't want you two trying to scratch each other's eyes out."

Margaret gave a fake cat yowl and made a scratching motion with her hand. It made me laugh, but there was something forced about the smile she gave me afterward.

Ruth must have sensed the awkwardness, too because she changed the topic. "We still on for the *I, Claudius* marathon tomorrow?" she asked Margaret.

"For sure," replied Margaret.

I, Claudius was a Roman period TV drama. I hadn't seen it before – it would be pretty cool to watch it with some friends. I didn't want to be pushy, though. Feeling left out, I started packing to leave. I threw my bag over my shoulder and I gave the girls a small wave. "I guess I'll see you guys next week."

"See you, Ally," said Margaret.

"Wait a sec, Ally," said Ruth, and I spun back around to face them. I saw Margaret and Ruth have the kind of one-second silent eyebrow conversation that only best friends could have. Then Ruth continued, "What are you doing tomorrow?"

I looked at the ceiling as if I was thinking hard. "Let's see. Manicure. Pedicure. Full body wax. Walk the dog …"

Margaret and Ruth laughed. I was showing off, for

sure, but I was really enjoying myself. I didn't get to play the clown around Cat. Being funny and outgoing was her job. It was cool to hang out with people I could show a different side to.

"You should come along tomorrow," Ruth said. "The plan is to watch the first six episodes of the series on DVD."

I knew it was about the Roman Emperor, Claudius, but not much more than that. "Sounds like fun! I've always wanted to watch it," I said enthusiastically.

Ruth gave me her address and told me to come by around ten. She also said they might invite a few other people – including James Whisker.

I was surprised at the way my stomach lurched when I heard this. *Get a grip*, I told myself. *He's just a boy*. Why was I suddenly so nervous about the possibility of seeing him?

"Actually, I was supposed to ask him this afternoon," Margaret admitted sheepishly. "But I chickened out."

"Don't worry," said Ruth. "I'll ask him later."

"Ruth and James live across the street from each other," Margaret explained.

I felt a strange little stab of jealousy. *Weird*. I decided to change the subject. "Should I bring some snacks?" I asked.

"That'd be great," replied Ruth.

"Don't bring cupcakes," said Margaret, with a warning glance. "*I'm* bringing cupcakes. James *loves* cupcakes."

Ruth gave her friend a cheesy smile. "The way to a man's heart …" she began.

"… is through his stomach!" Margaret concluded.

"Okay," I said slowly. It made me feel a bit weird that Margaret and James already had a … something … going on. Had I just imagined the connection between us in the library? "So what should I bring?"

"As long as it's not cupcakes," said Margaret, "it doesn't matter!"

Clearly Margaret didn't think I could bake anything to rival her cupcakes. Even though she was probably right, her comment did hurt my feelings a little. *Don't be silly, Ally*, I told myself. *Just suck it up and be positive.* I straightened up and plastered on a smile.

We said good-bye and as I was walking to the bus stop, I started thinking about what kind of culinary extravaganza I could whip up. One thing was certain, I was going to have to expand my cooking repertoire beyond toast and fried eggs. But what could I make? I wanted to impress James with something as lip-smacking as Margaret's cupcakes. But I wanted Margaret to adore me too. *Ugh!* I was wedged between my new friends and my new crush – I was in quite a jam. I turned the situation over in my mind until the bus arrived.

It was only as I boarded the bus that I realized I'd completely forgotten about Cat and her audition. The moment I sat down I pulled out my phone and composed a text:

Bet you blitzed that audition. Tell me everything!

After I pressed send, I kept my phone in my hand, hoping it'd start jumping with a reply. It didn't.

Chapter Eight

Early the next morning I flicked through my parents' cookbooks, desperate to find a delectable and unique dish that I could make for the *I, Claudius* marathon. While Mum and Dad were having breakfast, I trawled through the fridge, freezer and pantry for ingredients, searching for the perfect combination.

I had my heart set on Mum's famous fig tart, until I realized that I had no figs or almonds or tart shells. Then I thought I'd try croissants, but when I read the whole recipe it turned out that there were fifty-six steps to be completed – over three days. Besides, we had no yeast.

"Is there no food in this house?" I demanded.

"Someone got up on the wrong side of the bed," commented Dad from the breakfast table.

He was right, I was feeling quite grumpy. Cat still hadn't replied to my text asking how the audition had gone. She was definitely giving me the cold shoulder. Even though Dad was right, his comment made me grumpier than ever and I closed the fridge door a bit too roughly.

"Go easy," Mum said. "Ally, what are you looking for anyway?"

"Ingredients!" I cried dramatically.

Mum rolled her eyes. "Yes, but for what?"

"I have to take a plate of something to Ruth's place."

"I could run you down to the bakery," suggested Mum. "What about chocolate éclairs?"

"No, it has to be something homemade," I said.

Mum looked confused. "Why?"

Truly, I didn't know the answer myself. I knew I was in a flap about James and the fact that Margaret was going to woo him with cupcakes. Whether she knew it or not, we'd become fierce rivals, both trying to win James's heart via his stomach.

"Because homemade things taste better," I told Mum sweetly.

"Well, that depends who's making them," Mum replied dryly. "If you'd told me sooner, I could have gone shopping for ingredients and helped you cook something this morning."

"It's okay," I said, sighing deeply. "I think we've got everything I need to make a chocolate cake ..." I peered into the pantry. "Well, almost everything. We don't have any baking chocolate."

"You can use cocoa," said Mum. "It just won't be as rich." She came over to the pantry and pulled out a tin of cocoa powder. "There you go."

"Thanks." I took the tin.

Mum put her hand on my shoulder. "You know you could save yourself a lot of trouble by just buying something. No one expects a fourteen-year-old girl to whip up a chocolate cake just like that. We could buy something and you could just pretend you've made it.

We've all done that before. Every Christmas I put a frozen lasagna in the oven and tell Granny Motbey that I made it myself."

"I don't know. If it looks too professional, everyone will know I didn't make it."

"Then just be honest and tell people you bought it. No one will mind, Ally." Mum gave me a sideways hug. "Believe me."

I took a long, hard look at the tin of cocoa. Maybe Mum was right. Maybe no one would care whether I'd baked something myself. They'd probably even wish that I hadn't, if it turned out badly. Then I thought, *Margaret will probably prefer it if I bring something from a bakery, so her homemade cupcakes look even better.* It was a horrible thought, but I couldn't help thinking it. For some reason I really wanted to impress James.

Of course, it wasn't *only* James I wanted to impress. If I could show that I was good at Latin, a bit funny and made delicious food, I would prove to the girls how right they were to invite me into their group. I had to come up with the perfect dish.

Margaret had said that it didn't matter what I brought. Well, I *wanted* it to matter. I wanted James's attention. And I wanted the girls to be my new friends.

But was it worth risking a potentially disastrous bake-off? I couldn't decide.

If you think Ally should make a chocolate cake, go to page 255.

If you think Ally should buy treats from the bakery, go to page 268.

Ally TELLS CAT about her secret romance with Tony

Chapter Eight

When the bell rang for lunch, Cat wasn't waiting for me outside my French class like usual.

I wandered out into the quad and she was sitting on a bench, looking like she didn't have a care in the world. When she noticed me walking towards her, she smiled a smug little smile. I wondered for a moment whether she'd known I would come looking for her. I searched her smile for an answer. *Maybe.* But I also detected a slight look of relief.

"Cat, we need to talk," I said firmly. I was determined to have my say.

She jumped up lightly, looping her arm through

mine. "Let's walk and talk," she said, pulling me along beside her. "I need chocolate. To the cafeteria!"

"Cat …" I dug in my heels and brought us to a halt, wheeling her around to face me.

Cat sighed impatiently. "You're not still going on about this double date, are you? Really, you're being such a baby –"

"It's not about that," I said, interrupting her. "Well, it kind of is." I looked at her pleadingly. "Can we go somewhere private?"

I saw a flash of worry cross Cat's eyes. She pulled her arm from mine. "Sure," she said. "Is it something personal?"

"You could say that." My voice quavered and I actually had to bite my lip to stop myself from crying.

We went into the auditorium and I closed the double doors behind us. Then I took a seat in the back row of chairs.

Cat sat beside me, looking very serious and a bit uncomfortable. "What is it, Ally?"

I took a deep breath. Then the words gushed out

like water from a pressure hose. "Something happened between me and Tony."

Cat folded her arms, rubbing them with her hands, as though a cold breeze was blowing through the airtight auditorium. "Something more than just a singing lesson?" she asked.

"We kissed."

A strange little smile formed at the edge of Cat's mouth. "So it *wasn't* just a singing lesson. *I knew it!*" Then she gave an exaggerated shrug. "Okay, so you kissed ... Big deal."

"But it wasn't just last night," I confessed.

"What?" she asked, her eyes wide and slightly wild.

"It was last year," I rushed on. "You were on vacation in Europe with your parents. I was stuck here. Tony and I started to hang out. And there was a kiss. I mean, it was totally awkward and awful, and it was the reason we hardly spoke to each other until this week ..."

Cat blinked and shook her head in disbelief. "But ... that was, like, ages ago. Why didn't you tell me?"

"I–I," I stammered. "I just wanted to forget about it."

"I tell you *everything*," she said, looking betrayed.

"I know, and I –"

"Come on," she demanded. "Why didn't you tell me?"

Tears stung my eyes. "I don't know."

"You do so," accused Cat. "Tell me."

Tears were streaming down my face. This was exactly what I didn't want to happen. She was so aggressive. I just couldn't handle it.

"Cat – I ..." I put my hands over my hot face and tried to think. Why – *really* – hadn't I told her? "I didn't want you to turn it into some big deal," I said finally.

"Why would I do that?"

"I don't know," I said, the frustration clear in my voice. I took a deep breath. "I feel really bad about it now," I said honestly.

"*You* kept it a secret. *You've* turned it into this big deal." Cat pointed at me accusingly.

I had known she would be angry, but I wasn't prepared for this. I dropped my hands into my lap, completely exasperated. I wanted to scream.

But it was then, in that moment of anger, that I

realized why I had kept the thing with Tony a secret for so long. I could see it all so clearly now.

I took a deep breath and tried to speak calmly. "You *hate* it when I spend time with other people. You won't let me get close to anyone else. I can't even talk to anyone else without having to give you a blow-by-blow account of the conversation." I heard myself get louder and more hysterical. "You're just so ... so ..." I searched for the right word. "*Controlling!*"

For a few seconds I felt both powerful and relieved. I had been holding everything inside for so long. But the good feelings didn't last.

Cat's face crumpled, and she burst into tears.

Instantly, I felt terrible. "I'm sorry ..." I began.

"No," sobbed Cat. "It's true. I don't mean to do it. I just want you to stay my best friend."

I hadn't expected this. We were both crying now.

"You don't know what it's like for me ... I'm always terrified you're going to go off with someone else," sniffed Cat. "You're smarter than me. Much smarter. And I keep thinking you're going to ..." she paused to wipe her eyes "… you know, make friends with someone more clever and more interesting … and dump me."

I felt stunned. *Cat? Feeling vulnerable?* I could hardly believe what I was hearing. I reached for her hand. For a moment we just sat there, holding hands in silence.

"Don't be crazy," I croaked finally, squeezing her hand. "You'll always be my number one friend. I don't know anyone who's as fun as you … or as talented. I mean, when I hear you sing, I wonder why I bother trying hard at anything."

Cat smiled at me and squeezed my hand back.

"Besties forever?" she asked.

"Besties forever," I said gently. But I wanted to be totally honest with her. "And if we happen to have other friends too, that's okay. It doesn't mean we're going to abandon one another."

We sat quietly for a few moments. Then Cat asked, "So, was last night's kiss any better than the first one?"

I nodded, and felt a big smile work its way across my face.

Cat grinned mischievously. "Or should I just mind my own business?"

"It was amazing!" I mooned. "Now I know what all the fuss is about."

"Just as well it happened in Tony's room and not yours."

"What do you mean?"

"Um ... have you completely forgotten about the other man in your life?"

"Oh, Chris. Yeah. Well, he's never kissed me like that!"

Cat leaned over and gave me a huge hug. She held on really tight, like she thought I would disappear if she let go.

"No one could ever replace you," I assured her, hugging her back. And it was true. Cat might have been bossy and a little controlling, but she was my best friend and she always had my back, in her own special way.

That afternoon, instead of catching the bus, Cat and I walked home from school to give us maximum gossip time. There was enough time to tell her everything about the night before, including how I had sung practically in tune – and really loved it – and how I'd forced Tony to explain himself.

"I'm glad you stood up to him," said Cat. "Because if you hadn't, I would have. I mean, who did he think he was, just brushing you off last year?" She looked furious at the thought.

That, I thought, *was exactly what I was afraid of.*

"He's not like that anymore," I told her. "He's not a spineless wimp."

"Obviously not," said Cat with a knowing smile. "From now on, I'm going to look at Tony Rickson in a totally different light. I knew he liked you, but honestly – I didn't think he had it in him."

I walked her to her place first, and she dropped her bag by the front door. Then she walked me back to my place. As we walked up my driveway, Cat touched my arm to get my attention.

"What?"

"It's *him*."

And sure enough, there was Tony, sitting on his front porch with a guitar on his lap. I had a feeling he'd been waiting for me.

"Hey, Tony," said Cat.

"Hi," replied Tony. He strummed his guitar dorkily, which made me smile. "You girls weren't on the bus."

"We decided to walk," I explained. I felt my face get warm as I recalled what we'd been talking about the whole way home. I still felt very nervous around Tony. But I could tell he was nervous too – the way his eyes didn't settle on any one thing gave him away. For some reason his nervousness made me feel a teeny bit better.

"So I spoke to Ollie today ..." Tony started.

Cat looked delighted – and relieved. "Really?"

"... and he said he'd like to catch up. You know, the four of us."

"Cool!" piped Cat. She grinned, and then said something surprising.

"You know what? I've gotta go. Mum needs me to help her with ... er ... the laundry."

I looked at her, trying to figure out what she was

talking about. I don't think she had helped with the laundry once in her life.

She turned her face a little, so Tony couldn't see, and winked at me. "See ya," she said, turning on her heel and heading back across the street.

Tony waved to her, then turned his attention to me. "Have you got time for some more practice?" he asked, flicking his shaggy hair back with his hand.

"Sure," I replied, trying to play it cool. But I couldn't help smiling.

"Sit down." He gestured to the spot next to him on the porch.

"What? Here?"

"Yeah. Let's see how you do being accompanied by guitar."

I looked up and down the street, feeling a little embarrassed about the possibility of serenading my neighbors – well, except Tony.

As I sat down on the Ricksons' porch, I felt a huge sense of release. Not only had I finally been able to let Cat know how I felt, I had discovered how she had been feeling, too. I'd had no idea she was so scared of losing me. It was a bit ridiculous, and I hoped now she realized just how ridiculous it was. Maybe now we could both relax a little.

Ally KEEPS her romance with Tony a secret

Chapter Eight

My tall iced mocha stood untouched on the table. My stomach had been somersaulting since we'd arrived at the café, and puking on a double date was something I was keen to avoid.

Tony sat beside me, still and silent. He was perched squarely on his chair as if he was bolted to it. He hadn't touched his drink either.

Not wanting to upset Cat, and feeling guilty about my secret, I'd given in and agreed to the double date with Ollie and Tony. Now here we were, four teenagers hanging out in a fancy café after school.

Cat and Ollie were sitting across the table from us,

having the time of their lives. Cat was already wearing Ollie's school sweater, which he gave her when she complained about being cold. Never mind that her own sweater was squashed at the bottom of her schoolbag …

Now he was reaching in front of her to steal a piece of her jam croissant.

"Hey!" Cat shouted, slapping his hand away.

Ollie pulled his hand back dramatically, looking mock-devastated.

It was all a bit sickening to watch, to be honest. I turned to Tony. He raised his eyebrows and shrugged. I smiled quickly and looked away again, shaking my head. I felt too anxious to say anything, and the feeling seemed to be mutual. I wasn't sure whether he was feeling overshadowed by Ollie, or still edgy after last night. He hadn't been very talkative when he agreed to set up this date, but at least he had agreed to it. So he must like me a bit … I just couldn't tell!

But one thing I knew I could definitely count on was that Tony wasn't about to spill the beans to Cat. He was doing a good impersonation of a vault – safe and cold and silent. So, if my secret was safe, why did I feel so dreadful?

Ollie, who'd already downed a club sandwich and two strawberry milkshakes, was sneaking his hand back across the table towards Cat's afternoon snack.

"C'mon," he pleaded, begging like a dog as he eyed Cat's croissant. "I'm staaarving. Are you really going to let me *starve*?"

Cat tilted her head to the side. "Well, okay." She picked up the crunchy end of her croissant and held it up to Ollie's mouth.

He snatched it away with his teeth.

Cat yelped. "You *bit* me! Ow! Ow!" She clutched her fingers and held them to her chest.

"Oh no!" he cried. Croissant crumbs sprayed from his mouth onto the table. He grabbed Cat's injured hand and pulled it to his face so he could examine it. "Teeth marks!" He took her hand in his and kissed it quickly. "There. Made it better. I'm so sorry, Cat."

By now Cat was giggling. "It's okay, I'll live."

It had broken the ice a bit, and we all started

laughing. As Cat laughed and Ollie fussed over her hand, I felt myself relax. I pulled my drink towards me and took a sip.

When I looked over, Tony was doing the same. He smiled at me and rolled his eyes at the spectacle of Cat and Ollie.

I rolled my eyes back, but secretly I wished that Tony and I were having as much fun together. Ollie was so obviously rapt to be in Cat's company.

But then our knees knocked together under the table and my stomach leapt in delight. Tony grinned nervously at me and I sank into a fantasy about the two of us walking down the street holding hands.

I was so blissfully engrossed in my daydream that I didn't notice the café door open, even though it was right in front of me. I didn't register Louisa Andrews's presence until she was literally looming over our table, so close that she could have sucked the whipped cream off my mocha.

"Well, isn't this nice?" she hissed.

Ollie dropped Cat's hand onto the table. A look of dread came over his face.

Louisa smiled bitterly. "What are you doing with these grade 9 *losers*?" She gestured at Cat and me like we were roadkill.

"Aw, come on, Lou," said Ollie with a nervous laugh. "Don't be stupid. Sit down."

I was amazed that Ollie was still trying to be nice to her. *Why doesn't he tell her to go jump?*

Louisa tossed her orange ponytail over her shoulder. "I'd rather not." Then, after shooting Cat a look of utter contempt, she looked innocently at Ollie. "I'll just see you tomorrow at the movies."

I looked at Cat, aghast. *Movies?* I thought. What was going on?

A waitress came over to our table. "Can I get you something?" she asked Louisa.

"No thanks," Louisa replied icily. Then she turned to Cat. "I hope you're ready to be sung out of the auditorium tomorrow." Then she whirled around dramatically and stormed out of the café.

The bell on the door jangled as if celebrating her departure. All eyes shot to Ollie. He just let out a huge breath and stared into space, not saying anything.

I turned to Tony, who looked as confused as I felt. He shrugged, as if to say, *I don't know what's going on.* I wanted to believe him.

Cat, whose stormy expression showed just how unimpressed she was, said, "I didn't know you were going out with her, Ollie."

Ollie shook his head vigorously and held up his hands in a mock-surrender. "No, it's not like that! A whole group of us are going to the movies … after the audition. You know, to celebrate. She's not my girlfriend, I swear!" He looked pleadingly at Cat.

Cat just checked her watch. "We'd better get going, Ally," she said, in a dangerously calm voice. Cat laid a twenty dollar bill on the table, and I followed her out of the cafe.

"That was incredible!" I said breathlessly, honestly wishing I was capable of standing up to a guy like that. "You're amazing!"

We strode down the street, arm in arm, exchanging triumphant looks. But there was a slight niggle in the back of my mind. I thought for a moment. Ollie seemed pretty genuine. And he had been super affectionate with Cat. I couldn't remember a time when I'd seen him ever treat Louisa as more than a friend.

"Cat…" I began tentatively. "I kind of have a feeling he actually really likes you."

Cat slowed her pace. "Really?"

Then, as if on cue, we heard a shout behind us. "Cat!" called Ollie. The boys were running down the street after us.

We stopped, and Ollie came bounding up to Cat. He slipped his hands around her waist. "Hear me out," he began.

I didn't get to hear the rest because Tony grabbed me by the elbow and swept me off the sidewalk onto the grassy edge. I looked back at Cat to see if she was all right. She was listening intently to whatever Ollie was saying. Her coy smile said it all. I turned back to Tony.

His eyes were worried. "Ally, did I do something wrong?"

My heart melted. "You haven't done anything wrong," I replied.

"So what's up?"

I wasn't about to lie to him. I leaned close and whispered in his ear. "Cat doesn't know about … you know …"

"What?"

"She doesn't know about *us*. She doesn't know what's been happening."

"Oh." He looked confused for a moment. Then he brushed aside his hair and smiled. "So?"

"Well, I feel bad," I explained. "Cat and I tell each other *everything*."

Tony still looked confused. He just didn't seem to get it. Then he looked down, frowning slightly, and asked me a question that broke my heart. "Are you embarrassed by me?"

"No *way!*" I said. "I mean, I used to be embarrassed about what happened last year, but not anymore."

"Good. So you won't mind if I do *this*." He put his arm around my shoulders, pulled me close and kissed me quickly on the lips.

I reeled back, gasping. I grinned stupidly at Tony, then spun around to check whether Cat had seen.

She was pressed against a store window, lips locked against Ollie's. "Oh no way!" I squealed.

Tony laughed. "I think Cat's got other things on her mind."

I turned back to him and giggled. "Guess so."

"And, anyway, what happens between you and me is none of her business." He put his hands around my waist.

I stole one more glance at Cat and Ollie. They were kissing as if the world around them – including me – didn't exist.

"Maybe it isn't her business," I said. It was only as I said the words that I realized they were true.

Cat knew Tony and I liked each other – we were on a double date, for crying out loud! But did she really have to know every detail? Tony and I stood there on the grass gazing into each other's eyes. I could feel the world falling away from us. Why couldn't we keep a few things to ourselves?

"So," began Tony, with a cute grin. "How are you feeling about the audition tomorrow?"

"Still nervous."

"Want to come over to my place for some more practice?"

"Sure." I stepped back onto the sidewalk and called out, "Good-bye," to Cat. She just waved without looking.

"I think she'll be okay without you," said Tony, taking my hand.

Chapter Nine

I stepped onto the stage. Taking a deep breath, I tried to look beyond the faces. I knew that if I made eye contact with anyone, I would definitely laugh – or cry.

Just get through the next two minutes, I told myself. I was as ready as I was ever going to be.

In the privacy of Tony's room yesterday – door left ajar, for his mother's sake – I'd sung the melody of *Thumbs-up for the Spaniard* so many times that I couldn't get it out of my mind. I was practically on autopilot. There was no way I was going to choke or forget the words.

Tony was sitting at the piano a few feet away from me on the other side of the stage. He smiled and started playing the introduction just like he had for all the others, including Cat and her arch-nemesis, Louisa.

Cat had received a standing ovation for her audition. Louisa's had been good as well, but her nerves showed. Her voice was blow-your-hair-back loud and strangled by her over-the-top vibrato. Of course, I would have done anything to have such a powerful voice. I knew I'd be lucky to get through my audition more or less in tune, never mind my tone, timbre and diction.

I opened my mouth, tried not to worry too much about what came out, and before I knew it I was holding the final note. I tried to hear whether it clashed with the chord Tony was playing, but it was over too quickly.

There was a pause, and then scattered clapping. Louisa was in the front row clapping extra slowly. Cat let out a great whoop, and Ollie clapped his hands raucously above his head. Mrs. Carey wrote something on her notepad and her son, Paul, gave me the thumbs-up.

I felt pumped. I wasn't expecting a lead role of any kind, but I was pretty sure I could hold my own in the chorus.

I looked over at Tony and mouthed, *Thank you.*

He mouthed back, *You were great.*

Now I was looking forward to being part of *Gladiator: The Musical.* I knew that Tony's songs would bring it to life and save it from lameness. It was exciting. How could I ever have thought that the musical would be a drag?

On Sunday afternoon, Cat and I went for a long walk around the lake. Cat was alternately sweating over the audition and swooning over Ollie.

"We are going to be *the* couple of the musical this year," Cat said breathlessly.

"A very good-looking couple," I agreed.

Cat grinned slowly like she was soaking up the compliment. Then her face became serious.

"You know, Ally," she began, "being in a relationship is very stressful."

I tried not to laugh. Cat and Ollie had been together

for a total of three days.

"Don't get me wrong," she said. "I'm totally into Ollie. But I'm always worried. I mean, what if he loses interest? What if Louisa gets the part of Lucilla and he has to kiss her for the musical? He could fall in love with her …"

I shook my head. "Not going to happen."

"Which? Louisa's going to play Lucilla, or Ollie's never going to fall for Louisa?"

"Neither," I said decisively.

"You don't think he's got a thing for her?"

"No way!"

"You don't think she's more sophisticated than me? She *is* in grade 10."

Until now I hadn't really gotten how insecure Cat was. I felt sad that she was so worried Ollie would just go off her in a second. I put my hand on hers. "Cat, he's totally into you. Trust me."

Her face relaxed into a happy smile. Then, in a knowing tone, she said, "And you know who's into you?"

I feigned ignorance. "Who?"

"Tony Rickson. *Totally.*"

"Really?" I was having trouble keeping a straight face. The mention of his name sent a jolt of excitement through my body. I couldn't help thinking about our kiss.

Cat went on, oblivious. "Yup. Well, he spent all that time coaching you … and he was so keen to set up the double date."

I could barely stop myself from grinning, but I managed to keep an even voice. "Maybe he's just a nice guy. Maybe he just wanted to see you and Ollie get together. I mean you *are* going to be *the* couple of the musical …"

Cat shoved me in the shoulder gently. "Hey! Don't mock me."

"I'm sorry," I chuckled, "but you're so cute when you're in love."

"Shut up! But, seriously, what about Tony?" asked Cat. "He used to be nerdy, but he's improving with age. And we'll all be spending a lot of time together. My prediction: you two will be a couple by the first performance."

"And you would be okay with that?"

"Aren't you okay with me and Ollie?"

"Of course! I'm happy for you!"

Cat's face came over serious for just a moment. "I guess I'd be happy for you too then."

"We'll see ..." I replied cagily.

Cat broke back into her rascally smile. "Admit Tony's a hunk!"

I rolled my eyes. "I'm not admitting anything."

Conversation drifted to other topics – music, Cat's latest favorite reality show, Ollie, and then Ollie again. It was so nice to spend the weekend in the park with Cat. Things felt good between us at the moment. I knew she'd cotton on to my thing with Tony Rickson at some point. But in the meantime I kind of liked having him all to myself!

Ally tells CAT *exactly* WHAT she *thinks*

Chapter Eight

For what seemed like forever I had bitten my tongue and allowed my best friend to rule over me, to crush and cajole me, but now … Well, now I was furious.

Standing at the back of the auditorium, with my back to the double doors, I roared, "Hey, *Cat*!"

She spun around in her seat. And so, for that matter, did everyone else. Mrs. Carey shook her head and raised her hands in exasperation.

I had so much to say, but with an audience of a hundred fellow students, plus one cranky music teacher, I choked. The auditorium went silent.

"Um, Cat," I squeaked, suffering an extreme bout

of stage fright. "Could I please see you outside?"

Cat stood and stared at me.

"For goodness' sake, girls," barked Mrs. Carey. "Either stay or go, but please stop disrupting this audition with your … your … *theatrics*!"

I walked out of the auditorium, then looked through the little windows in the doors. As Cat came down the aisle, everyone turned to stare.

I stepped back as the doors were flung open like the doors of a saloon. Cat appeared before me, glowering. She let the doors swing shut and then stood with her arms folded. That's when I realized this was going to be a showdown.

"What?" she demanded.

"You made a fool of me in there!" I shout-whispered. "I can't believe you told everyone about Chris!"

Cat shifted her weight from one foot to the other, as if she wasn't quite sure she should have done it either.

I kept going. "You don't actually know as much about my love life as you think. For one thing, I don't need imaginary boyfriends. I had a *real* one last year.

Yeah, that's right! While you were gallivanting around Europe with your parents, I was hanging out with Tony Rickson ... and it was awesome. And we *kissed*. And I didn't breathe a word because I knew how silly you'd be about it. You can't *stand* it when I spend time with someone else, or even like someone else. Well, guess what? I *like* Tony."

Cat was silent, but her eyes were blazing, and I knew her mind was racing. "Is that all?" she said finally.

"Good luck with your audition, Cat," I said sarcastically. "I'd rather be locked in an elevator with Louisa Andrews for three hours than audition for the musical with you!" And with that, I spun on my heel and marched out of the school building. I didn't look back.

I walked all the way home, feeling wildly triumphant and self-righteous. But by the time I reached my room, I just felt drained. I flung myself onto my bed, where Chris Hemsworth – no longer a secret friend – mooned down at me. After what Cat had said, I couldn't even look at him, let alone speak to him. I climbed onto my bed and, with a single grab, pulled the poster off the ceiling. I watched crumpled Chris float to the floor.

With a wave of anger, I grabbed my bag and poured everything out of it, looking for my phone. I wanted to see whether Cat had texted me to apologize yet. There were no messages.

I collapsed onto my bed again and burst into tears. I must have cried myself to sleep because the next thing I knew it was dark and Mum was shaking me awake for dinner.

"I'm not hungry," I told her truthfully. "I feel sick."

"Hmm. That's what Tony Rickson said."

I sat up. The mention of his name made me feel nervous and excited.

"What do you mean? When?"

"He came over about half an hour ago, but I told him you were sleeping. He said that you weren't yourself at school today. Is that right?" Mum sat on the edge of my bed and stroked my hair.

"I don't know," I replied, picking up my pillow and hiding my face in it. "I guess so."

"Well, he was worried, but he said he'd see you

tomorrow. You know, Ally …" Mum paused "… I think he might have a crush on you."

"Hmm," I groaned into my pillow, feeling an odd mix of embarrassment and happiness.

I peeked up to see what Mum was doing. She was bending over to pick up something off the carpet. It was my poster. She held it up and smiled. "Not into hunks anymore, Ally?"

I grunted.

"Do you want me to chuck it in the trash?"

"Nah," I said quickly, sitting up. She handed it to me and I laid it on my bed.

"Well, darling," she said, giving me a quick hug. "Dinner's on the table if you're up to it."

"Maybe later," I mumbled.

After Mum left, I changed into my PJs and went into the kitchen. My parents were at the table, talking. There was a place set for me. I sat down.

"It walks!" Dad goofed gently. "Everything okay?"

"I had a fight with Cat," I said simply.

"Do you want to talk about it?" Mum asked.

"Not really," I said, but then I realized that I kind of did want to talk about it.

"I think maybe I've changed," I said. "And I'm not sure I want to be best friends with Cat anymore."

Mum and Dad looked at each other.

"Sometimes," began Mum, "friends outgrow each other. You and Cat have been in each other's pockets for a long time. Maybe it's time to … pursue new friendships."

I sighed, wondering who I would pursue new friendships with, and how.

We sat in silence for a few minutes, eating dinner. Then I thought I heard piano music coming from next door. I got up and went to the kitchen sink to open the window.

With the window open, I could make out the tune quite clearly. It was a song Tony and I had listened to during our walks through Cherrywood Lakes last year. It was *Ho Hey* by The Lumineers. I knew that he could only have been playing it for me.

Blushing, I returned to the dinner table. It was the

most romantic thing anyone had ever done for me. Then I heard a faint message beep from my phone, which was in my room, but I didn't move. I stayed at the table, listening to the song with a swelling heart.

Ally BITES her tongue about Cat

Chapter Eight

Head hanging low, I left the auditorium. I felt totally humiliated. The tension between Cat and me had been building for a while, but nothing could have prepared me for a public outburst like that. And all because I'd finally been honest with her about not wanting to do the stupid musical …

All I could think was, *She'd better apologize.* There was no way I'd be crawling back to her after this. We'd had some fights before, but never on this scale. Cat was going to have to say sorry – and really mean it.

Walking the empty halls, I felt really alone. The only classes I had without Cat were French because she took

Italian, and math, because she was in a different math class. Sure, I was friendly with some people, but they never came to sit with us at lunch or recess and we never went to each other's houses. Whenever I'd started hanging out with someone new at school, Cat woud always muscle them out. I could tell everyone thought that Cat and me were an exclusive twosome. It annoyed me a bit, but I never felt I could do anything about it. And now without Cat, I had no one.

Trudging down the hallway, I started to think about who I could try to be friends with. Who was as bubbly and funny and mischievous as Cat? Who would make me laugh, and drag me along on their adventures? I couldn't think of one person. There was a reason Cat was my best friend. I was quiet and creative and quirky on the inside. Cat was loud and brash and wore her emotions on the outside. Together we had a great time ... until recently. I was beginning to wonder if we understood each other at all. If we were so close, then why hadn't I been able to tell her about Tony Rickson? Sure, I was *so* over him now, but for a few months last year he'd been all I could think about. And I'd felt like I couldn't breathe a word of it to Cat …

I was turning all this over in my mind as I passed the Latin classroom. At first I walked right on by, but then I remembered the extension class and I turned back to peek in through the little glass square in the door. I felt sad that I had thrown away this opportunity, just to keep Cat happy.

I could see Mrs. Hawkins sitting on the edge of her desk. A dark-haired girl in the front row was reading out loud from a sheet. Everyone else was quiet, looking down at the papers on their desks. It was the opposite of the raucous scenes in the auditorium.

I wished I could go in and join them, but I knew I couldn't. What if Mrs. Hawkins turned me down in front of all those grade 10s? I'd die of humiliation. *No, I thought to myself. I've suffered enough embarrassment for one afternoon.*

I dragged myself from the window and continued up the hall. I'd only gone a few feet when I heard a noise behind me.

"Ally?" It was Mrs. Hawkins.

I stopped and turned around.

"I thought I saw you at the door," she said.

"Oh, I'm just on my way home," I explained.

"Is the musical audition over already?"

I shook my head sheepishly.

"Decided to give it a miss?"

"You could say that," I replied. Then, blushingly, I admitted, "I wasn't actually that keen on auditioning in the first place. I think I was doing it for the wrong reasons."

Mrs. Hawkins nodded. Then she seemed to read my mind. "It's not too late to join us in here, you know. We've nearly finished for today, but I'm running the class until the end of term."

I couldn't hide my joy. "So I could come next Friday?"

"Why don't you come in now and catch the end of the class? I'll introduce you to the group."

I hesitated for just a moment, the horrible scene in the auditorium still fresh in my mind. What if they didn't like me? What if they laughed at me?

Mrs. Hawkins must have seen the fear on my face because she said, smiling, "They don't bite, Ally."

I followed her into the classroom, shutting the door behind me.

Mrs. Hawkins faced the class. "Everyone, this is Ally Motbey from grade 9. She'll be joining us on Fridays."

I gave a small, lame wave, feeling slightly awkward. A few people called, "Hi."

Then Mrs. Hawkins gave me a bundle of papers and I went to the only empty seat, which was in the back row. The guy next to me turned and grinned.

"Hey, Ally," he said. His blue eyes smiled behind his glasses. "I'm James."

I looked down at the papers then quickly stole another glance at James. He seemed to be in the process of stealing a glance at me.

"Ah ... we're up to the third page now," he explained.

I turned to the third page. James reached over and pointed to a paragraph down at the bottom.

"If you need help with the vocab," he whispered, "just ask."

"Or I could just look at the vocab list at the top of the page," I replied, smiling.

James chuckled. "Wow, you really are as smart as Mrs. Hawkins says."

Suddenly Mrs. Hawkins was looming over my desk.

"Ally, I had to tell you and Cat off for talking during class. Don't tell me I'm going to have the same problem with James as well."

"Sorry," I said sheepishly. "I'll be quiet."

"Good," said Mrs. Hawkins. Then she leaned towards me and whispered into my ear, "I'm glad you're making some new friends."

I glanced at James.

"Me too," I said.

Ally CONFRONTS Cat

Chapter Nine

"Excuse me, guys, but I have to talk to Cat." Speaking through gritted teeth, I grasped the fleshy part of Cat's upper arm.

"Hey!" shrieked Cat, trying to pull away.

I was determined, though. I hauled her away from the surprised faces of her posse, and by the time I'd manhandled her as far as the lockers, she'd given up resisting. Once we were out of sight of the audition crowd, I let go and turned to face her.

"What's going on, Cat? Why are you acting like this?"

Cat folded her arms across her chest and glared at me. "I don't know what you're talking about."

"Yes, you do!" I hissed. "You're mad about my Latin extension class."

"I couldn't care less about your stupid Latin class," Cat replied, but with too much anger for someone who genuinely couldn't have cared less.

"Why are you ignoring me, then?"

"I didn't know you were going to turn up at the audition."

I glared at her for a moment and then I let her have it. "You've been a total cow to me ever since I told you I wasn't going to do the musical audition. You're lucky I showed up at all."

Cat's hands flew to her hips. "*I'm* lucky that *you* showed up?"

"Yeah. I could have gone straight home."

"Ally, you promised me you were coming to the audition. Then you broke your promise. Why should I be grateful for anything?"

"I had a terrible time at Latin," I confessed, my voice trembling with the memory of the entire class cackling and jeering.

"That's not my fault! You should have kept your promise." Cat's green eyes blazed with accusation.

In a way, she was right. I *had* broken a promise. But it was only because a fantastic opportunity had come up. Something I actually wanted to do – and that I had hoped I would be really good at.

I tried to explain it to Cat, hoping I could make her understand. "I … you … I thought I should … well … I thought I should go and do something I was good at. Instead of making an idiot of myself at an audition. Couldn't you tell that I didn't really want to do the musical?"

It was clear from the look on her face that she hadn't figured that out.

"I'm sorry, Cat," I said gently. "I shouldn't have promised something I wasn't sure I wanted to do."

Cat's expression and body language softened. She let her hands fall from her hips. "Okay. You're right. I've been a cow, and I'm sorry too."

I nodded, relieved. Things still seemed far from smoothed over, though. It was as if Cat had taken me on an emotional roller-coaster ride, and I was still feeling queasy from it. I tried to gather my thoughts.

"We don't have to do everything together, you know," I told her sincerely. "It doesn't make us any less best friends."

Cat nodded, her eyes shining with tears. "I know that now," said Cat. "At first I was really scared of having to do the musical without you."

"You shouldn't be." I had to bite the inside of my lip to stop my own tears.

"But I'm not anymore. I've realized that I *can* make other friends. They might not be as good as you, but ..."

"Well, I am a hard act to follow!" I said with a smile. We both giggled.

Without another word, Cat and I stepped into a hug.

"You *were* happy to see me when I walked into the auditorium this afternoon, weren't you?" I said, my chin resting on her shoulder.

"Yeah, of course," she said, sniffing. "But I was pretending not to be."

"Even your acting skills can't fool me," I told her.

"I still know you better than anyone else."

We pulled apart and smiled at each other.

"So tell me what happened in your Latin class," Cat said, smiling warmly.

"OH ... MY ... " I began.

"Give me your honest opinion, Ally," Cat said. "Who's the hottest guy on the field?"

I rolled my eyes. "It's Ollie, okay? Ollie, hands down. Happy?" I sounded annoyed, but I was smiling.

It was so nice to be hanging out with my bestie again. Somehow I felt like all the drama of the last few days had blown away, and now the sun was shining on our friendship – and it was brighter than ever.

Cat slipped her arm through mine. "Yes!" she squealed. "There are other hotties out there, though. I've got my eyes peeled."

We were standing on the sidelines of Cherrywood Field, where Cherrywood High and Penscombe Boys

Grammar were playing a soccer match. It was cold and windy, so we were piled up with scarves, gloves and beanies. I had a heavy wool coat on that my dad had bought when he was on a work trip overseas. I was completely toasty.

There was plenty of talent on the field – and I wasn't just talking about soccer. "Hey, there's Paul on the Penscombe team," said Cat. She waved and shouted, "Go, Paul!"

"Shhh!" I hissed. "Don't, Cat. You'll distract him."

But it was too late – Paul paused and looked over to the sideline to see who had called out. The ball whistled past his head and straight into the Penscombe goal. Cheers went up among the Cherrywood team and fans. The Penscombe guys groaned and dropped to their knees.

"Come on, Carey," shouted the Penscombe coach, a tall, gruff, gray-haired man in a jersey. "*De*-fense. You're off with the fairies."

"Off with the ladies, more like it," called a parent from the sidelines.

Paul was looking around in a daze, still trying to work out what had happened. Then his eyes came to rest on Cat and me. He put his hands on his hips in mock outrage. "Was that you two calling out?"

Cat nodded and I shook my head.

He narrowed his eyes and pointed at us. "Look, guys," he said to his teammates. "These are Cherrywood High's secret weapons."

"Eyes on the ball, Carey!" called the coach. Then he looked down the sideline at us. "And no more mischief from the Cherrywood crowd!"

For a moment it felt like all eyes were on us, and we both shrank deeper into our scarves and coats, giggling. To my relief, the referee blew his whistle and the match started again.

"Paul's cute, don't you think?" Cat whispered into my ear.

"He's all right," I replied.

"Oh, just all right, is he?" she teased, elbowing me gently in the side. "Wow, this James must be really something."

I'd finally had the opportunity to tell Cat about James and what had happened in the library and in Latin class. After much discussion and analysis, Cat had reached the definitive conclusion that he totally liked me. I wasn't so sure.

"*Brr*, it's cold," said Cat, stamping her feet. "I don't know how much longer I can be out here, hotties or no hotties."

"Maybe we could run laps of the field," I joked.

"I've got a better idea," she replied. "Let's go and get a sausage sandwich."

We walked around to the other side of the field, where a barbecue and a few folding tables had been set up. The wind blew the irresistible smell of barbecued beef sausages into our faces.

"Good idea," I told Cat as we joined the line.

When we got to the front of the line, I gasped when I saw who was manning the barbecue. Tongs in hand, turning sausages and wearing an apron with the words "Never trust a skinny chef" written on it, was none other than James Whisker himself.

After my speedy exit from Latin class yesterday, I wasn't exactly sure how things would be between us the next time we met. I was about to find out.

"Hey, Ally," he said casually, as if I'd never made a fool of myself at all.

Cat, who was still attached to me by linked elbow, gave me a huge nudge.

"Hey, James," I said shyly. Then I added, "This is my bestie, Cat."

"Hello, Cat," he said, waving the tongs at her.

"Hi, James. I've heard a lot about you," Cat said knowingly, and I died a little inside.

James shot me a curious look, his eyebrows raised.

"Um, I didn't know you'd be here," I said awkwardly.

He took off his glasses and rubbed his eyes with his forearm. "*Ugh!* My glasses keep fogging up."

I tried not to giggle. Watching him battling with the smoke and his fogged-up glasses decided it. *James was totally dorky – and totally cute.*

"It's hot behind the barbecue," I said, and was immediately embarrassed.

"Yeah," agreed Cat suggestively. "It's smokin' hot."

"So," said James, replacing his glasses and blinking through the smoke. "Can I offer you a smokin' sandwich?"

"Sure," I said.

"Me, too," cooed Cat.

The whistle sounded while James was preparing our sandwiches and all the soccer players, including Ollie, swarmed the barbecue. We snatched our food from the table in the nick of time.

"Hey, thanks! I'm starving," Ollie said to Cat, grabbing at her sausage sandwich. I had to admit even when he was sweaty and covered from head to toe in mud, he was still pretty swoon-worthy. Cat offered him her sandwich. But Ollie didn't take it. He just put his arm around her shoulder. "Thanks, babe, but I can buy my own."

Cat looked up at him with huge, admiring eyes. "So did you win the match?"

"Yeah," replied Ollie. "By one point."

Paul Carey wandered up and Cat introduced me. When the boys both got their sandwiches, we moved away a bit and stood talking and shivering under a tree.

For a second I glanced back at James, who was swamped by hungry, cold people. He was turning sausages like a madman.

Suddenly, Ollie blurted out, "Cat, you got the lead role in the musical."

"Ollie!" shouted Paul. "Man, you really can't keep a secret."

Cat grabbed my arm and we both started jumping up and down. "I can't believe it!" she squealed.

"I knew it!" I squealed back, my grin just as wide.

Ollie covered his ears and grimaced at Paul. "Ugh, why do they have to make that noise?"

When Cat and I had stopped jumping, Paul said, "Hey, who's that guy at the barbecue?"

Ollie looked over his shoulder. "That's James Whisker. He's a nerd, but he's okay."

"I think he's cute," said Cat, with a cheeky grin. "He's got nice eyes."

"He keeps looking over here," said Paul, and then added in a syrupy, high-pitched voice, "*with his nice eyes.*" He and Ollie laughed.

When the conversation moved back to the musical, I stole a peek over at the barbecue. James *was* looking at me. He tilted his head, as if to say, *Come over here*. I waited a moment or two before excusing myself and going back to the barbecue.

When I got there, James was cleaning up, putting leftovers and napkins into a big garbage bag. I automatically started clearing things and putting them in the bag. *Maybe he just wanted help packing up?* I thought.

"Fraternizing with the enemy?" James asked finally.

I stared at him blankly. Was he making fun of me?

Then he added, "The Penscombe guy."

"Oh, Paul? He's not the enemy. He's Mrs. Carey's son."

All of a sudden James seemed very nervous. He started shifting from foot to foot. "Is he your boyfriend?"

"No way!" I replied, laughing. "I mean, no. My friend Cat is going to be in the school musical. And, um, I don't have a boyfriend."

"So … I guess you're free to … go out with me?" He trailed off, then looked at me with a hopeful but worried smile. "You know, if you want?"

I didn't know what to say. I'd never been asked out before, not properly like this. So I just said, "Okay."

James's face burst into a huge smile. "Great! Maybe we could go for a walk in the park after school on Monday. We could look at the next bunch of poems Mrs. Hawkins gave us …"

I gazed up at him with an awkward smile and we both cracked up.

"I was going to ask you yesterday," said James. "But you left class so quickly, I didn't get a chance."

My face started burning. I put my palms up to cover my cheeks. "I had to go. I was so embarrassed! I had to get out of there."

"Why?"

"Ugh! Because of my total Furius fail. Why else?"

"Ally," James said, looking down at me with those piercing blue eyes. "All the poems were really hard and almost everyone messed up their lines. It's just that your mistake was really funny. I actually thought you'd done it on purpose. Then you went all quiet and I realized you'd made an honest mistake."

"I don't know if I can go back," I said, sounding whiny. "Everyone must think I'm a total fraud."

"Don't be crazy." James grinned his gorgeous smile and looked totally amused. "Everyone thought you were hilarious, especially because Mrs. Hawkins had been talking you up so much. It was totally epic."

"Really?"

"Imagine what a boring afternoon it would have been without you."

I stared up at him, wondering whether he'd just taken some pill that made him say all the right things. He gazed down at me.

"Hey, James," I said.

"What?"

"Your glasses are fogging up."

Laughing, he reached around and tugged my braid.

The End

Ally IGNORES Cat

Chapter Nine

"Ally, I hate to tear you away from your books, but you can't stay at home. The exterminator's coming to spray the house for cockroaches." Mum was standing in my doorway, all dressed up like she was going somewhere fancy.

I was on my bed with pages of Catullus poems, English translations and Latin textbooks spread around me. Theoretically, I was brushing up on my vocab to avoid any more embarrassing mistakes in class. But the truth was, I was doing a lot more sulking than studying.

I'd stormed off from the auditorium yesterday afternoon. Cat didn't even seem to notice me leaving, and she certainly didn't try to stop me — just as I'd expected.

Luckily Chris Hemsworth had done a great job of consoling me from the ceiling.

"Sorry, what?" I asked Mum.

"I said, the exterminator's coming so you can't stay here. He was meant to come yesterday while we were all out, but he got held up. We have to stay out of the house until this afternoon."

"Oh." I closed my Latin dictionary. "Well, I guess I'll just go to …" I'd been about to say "Cat's place," but of course that was out of the question "… to the park."

"What? All day? Ally, no. You can come with us. The Caves have invited us to lunch."

Mr. Cave was Dad's boss. The Caves didn't have any kids, and every time I'd visited them with Mum and Dad I'd been bored out of my mind.

"Do I have to, Mum?"

"Don't be silly, Ally. I'm sure the Caves won't mind. Bring your homework with you."

"Well, okay," I said grumpily.

"Wear something nice."

"Yes, Mum."

When she was gone, I looked up at Chris. "I'd rather stay here with you," I said glumly.

It turned out we weren't going to the Caves' place at all. They had arranged to take my parents to the Whitewater Yacht Club. It was an exclusive club that you couldn't join unless about a hundred other members of the club gave you a glowing character reference. (My parents were only allowed in as the Caves' guests!)

The club was right on the waterfront. There were rows and rows of huge, flashy yachts moored nearby. As we walked up to the club, I watched the yachts bobbing around on the dark, choppy waves the wind was whipping up, and banging against the pier. I was pretty sure that the Caves didn't actually own a yacht, but figured they must like going to the club to check out everyone else's.

When we arrived, I could tell from the look on Mrs. Cave's face that they hadn't expected my parents to bring me along. She smiled quickly and then pursed her mouth like she'd just sucked on a lemon. "No under-sixteens, I'm afraid," she said with a flick of her perfectly blow-dried blond bob. Then she pointed to a sign near the counter that confirmed it.

"That's okay," I said, actually relieved not to have to sit through lunch with those crashing bores. "I'll go and sit on the wharf."

"Perhaps we should go somewhere else for lunch," Mum suggested.

"No," I said quickly. "I'll be fine. Honest."

"Well, there's a takeout place a little further down the wharf," Dad said. "They do great fish-and-chips."

Dad gave me some money and then I headed outside.

It was very windy out on the wharf, so I walked quickly down to the fish-and-chips shop. There were plastic tables and chairs inside. It was warm and seemed like a good place to get some work done. I ordered my lunch, unpacked my backpack and, surrounded by books, started reading.

That was when the strangest thing happened. The tallest, most beautiful woman I'd ever seen walked into the restaurant. I thought I recognized her, but she was wearing a beret and huge, dark sunglasses, so I couldn't put my finger on exactly who she was. It was only when she spoke, to order her grilled fish and salad, that I realized whose company I was in.

"Linda Paice!" I said aloud, then covered my mouth. To my embarrassment, she turned around. She flipped her sunglasses onto her head.

"Do I … er … know you?" she asked.

"I'm a huge fan," I gushed. "And my best friend, Cat … well, *Supermodel Scout*'s her favorite show."

Linda gave me a dazzling smile, then turned back to the counter to pay for her order. I felt like a complete idiot. She was probably sick to death of strangers coming up to her and saying, "Oh, you're Linda Paice," as if she didn't already know. I looked down at my Latin books, but it was just for show. There was no way I could study with her in the room.

"What's that? Italian?"

I looked up to see Linda standing right next to me.

"Um … Latin, actually."

"Looks hard," she said.

"It's not that bad once you understand the rules."

"Like most things," she replied. I couldn't believe how friendly she was. It was only because she was already being so nice that I plucked up the courage to ask for a photo with her.

"Um … would you mind …" I began, pulling out my phone.

"A selfie? Sure. That would be fun."

She must get asked to pose in selfies about a million times a day. I felt bad adding to the selfie count, but she didn't seem to mind.

I stood up and we posed for the photo. Next to Linda, with her long legs, perfectly blow-dried hair and flawless olive skin, I must have looked like a mess. Still – she was Linda Paice!

"You can send that to your best friend," she said as I slipped my phone back into my pocket.

"My best friend?"

"Your friend who loves the show … it's a shame she's not here, actually. We're filming next door in the yacht club."

"Really?"

"Yeah. You should come and watch. Call your friend. Get her down here as well."

I thought for a moment. Watching a taping of *Supermodel Scout* would be a dream come true for Cat. But then, she hadn't been very nice to me lately. I honestly wondered whether I owed it to her to tell her about the taping.

"Actually," I said to Linda, "Cat and I, we're not getting along at the moment."

Linda looked sympathetic. "Really? What happened?"

"Five minutes on the grilled fish," the guy behind the counter called out.

Linda nodded, and sat down next to me.

"Well," I said, wondering where to start. "She's been freezing me out for a while. And then at school the other day, she put me down in front of a big group of people. It was really embarrassing."

Linda shook her head. "Life's too short to surround yourself with people like that," she said. "You're better off on your own."

"She isn't always like that, though," I said, thinking that being on my own didn't sound like much fun.

"Sounds to me like you're making excuses for her. Maybe it's time you started scouting for some new talent in the friend department."

I grinned at her joke. "Maybe."

Soon our fish-and-chips were ready. I scooped up my food – along with an armful of Latin books – and followed Linda out onto the wharf.

"Seriously," she said as we strutted along side by side, "if there's one thing show business has taught me, it's the value of good friends. Good friends tell you the truth, but they don't run you down in front of other people."

I was fast realizing that Cat hadn't been a good friend lately. Certainly not good enough to be my bestie.

We reached the yacht club and walked right in. Nobody tried to stop me.

"Good afternoon, Miss Paice," said the concierge. "Your personal assistant is looking for you."

"I was just picking up some lunch," replied Linda. "The best grilled fish in the city."

I followed her up a staircase and past the main dining room. As we passed the dining room, Mrs. Cave did such a big double take that her French roll began to untwist. I grinned as we kept walking to another huge room with a vaulted ceiling and a glass wall on the harbor side. There were cameras and sound and lighting equipment everywhere, and in the corner, sitting at a long makeup table with their sleek hair clipped up, were ten gorgeous models, some as young as me.

A small, skinny man with a pencil-thin moustache came rushing up to us.

"Linda, oh my, Linda – we're about to start! Time for your makeup!"

Linda turned to me. "Make yourself at home," she said, as the man with the moustache took her elbow and led her to the makeup table. "Sorry, I didn't get your name ..."

"It's Ally!" I called after her. "Ally Motbey."

I found a chair by the lighting equipment and opened my fish-and-chips. Then I spent the afternoon watching the models learn how to pose in a photo shoot and work with a photographer, all while the TV cameras were rolling. Linda was an amazing host, and I kept thinking about what she'd said about good friends. The weird thing was, I had a great time sitting there by myself. And I realized that whatever happened with Cat, I would be okay. I was fine without her.

The End

Ally MAKES a chocolate cake

Chapter Nine

I had exactly one hour before I had to leave for Ruth's. In that time I had to have a shower, get dressed, and bake a cake that needed forty-five minutes in the oven.

I got to work. I'd never tried to make a cake before, but how hard could it be?

I had Mum's cookbook on the counter, open at the chocolate cake recipe. The recipe called for real chocolate, but we didn't have any, so I decided to use cocoa powder instead, like Mum had suggested.

As I was pulling the flour out of the pantry, Mum stuck her head around the kitchen door. "Have you preheated the oven?" she asked.

I looked at the oven, cold and dark and still. "I was just about to," I replied huffily, rushing to the oven to turn it on.

"What about the cake pan? Have you lined and greased it yet?"

"I was just about to," I muttered.

"Baking paper's in the cupboard above the microwave," said Mum.

"*Okay*, Mum." She was making me nervous. "I'm on a time line here, you know."

Mum flashed a quick smile before retreating. I noticed her handbag on the kitchen counter. My mum's a hopeless chocoholic and I knew she always kept a packet of little chocolate squares in her bag.

It gave me an idea.

I dived into her handbag and pulled out a ziplock bag filled with chocolate squares. *Bingo!* I shook about half into my hand. Then, after checking the steps of the recipe again, I dropped the chocolate in a bowl with a stick of butter and melted them in the microwave. Surely the cake would taste better if I used real chocolate.

In no time at all I'd mixed the ingredients together and was pouring the mixture into the pan.

"On schedule?" asked Mum, coming back into the kitchen.

I looked at my watch. "Ahead."

"When do you want me to drop you off?"

"In exactly forty-five minutes," I replied with a grin.

An hour later I was walking up the driveway at Ruth's house, proudly carrying the chocolate cake on a plate and trying desperately not to drop it. I was dressed in my best outfit – skinny jeans and a tight-fitting, cable-knit sweater.

Margaret was waiting on the front doorstep, holding a container. "Hey, Ally," she said, eyeing my cake. "You've come prepared."

"It's not very Roman," I said with a grin. "But who doesn't love chocolate cake?"

Ruth let us in, and with a fluttering tummy, I

followed the girls into the family room. A girl I'd never met before was sitting on the couch. Ruth introduced us. "This is my friend Jessica. We went to primary school together."

"Chocolate cake – my favorite!" said Jessica.

There was a table set up in the corner of the room with a few plates of food and bottles of soft drinks on it. I put my cake down and watched as Margaret put out some vanilla cupcakes with strawberry frosting. I felt an uncomfortable but exciting sense of competition with her. I wondered if the same thoughts were going through her mind.

This was different from the rivalry Cat had with Louisa Andrews. Margaret was fun and nice and I wanted to be friends with her, so that made the situation even trickier.

Ruth got out the DVD and started pressing buttons on the remote. James hadn't arrived yet, but it seemed like we were starting without him. As the DVD menu came up on the screen, I said, to no one in particular, "So, are we all here?"

Ruth smiled. "I think so."

Jessica chuckled. "Put your hand up if you're not here."

We all raised our hands halfheartedly and everyone laughed.

I was going to have to be less subtle. "Didn't you invite that guy from Latin?" I asked Ruth.

"James?" she asked.

I tried to sound casual. "Yeah."

"He said he had to go to a soccer match today," said Ruth.

"Oh." It was hard to hide my disappointment. "He plays soccer?"

"Nope. He's working the sausage stand," she explained.

"Pretty lame excuse," said Margaret dejectedly.

Ruth shrugged. "His loss." Then she cleared her throat. "Now, does anyone have anything else to say before I start the first episode? Say it now or forever hold your peace."

"Actually," said Jessica, "I don't think I can sit here and look at that chocolate cake for the next hour. Can I have a slice now?"

"And me," said Margaret. "Let's see what you're made of, Ally." She was smiling, but I felt that sense of competition between us.

"Sure," I said, jumping to my feet. I cut two slices from the cake and handed them out. I was too edgy to eat, but I enjoyed watching the others wolf it down.

"This is amazing," said Jessica. "What's your secret?"

I pictured the chocolate squares I'd pilfered from Mum's handbag. "Real chocolate," I replied. "Good-quality stuff."

"Best chocolate cake I've ever tasted," said Jessica.

I couldn't believe it. Obviously I'd been far too hard on myself. I was brimming with pride.

"Okay, okay," said Ruth, as if she'd been wrestling with temptation. "Cut me a slice, Ally." I passed her a slice and watched her eyebrows shoot up as she took a bite. "Not bad!" she said.

Finally, we began the first episode and I settled on the couch next to Margaret. I could smell her perfume. I wondered if she was as disappointed as I was that James had chosen the company of sausages over us.

It was about half an hour into *I, Claudius* when I noticed that Jessica was wriggling in her seat. I wondered whether she was bored. But there wasn't much time to wonder because she suddenly stood up, grabbing her stomach and looking queasy. "Excuse me," she gasped, and sprinted out of the room as though her life depended on it.

"I hope she's okay," I said to Ruth.

"Don't worry," Margaret reassured me. "She's not into Roman history like we are."

Ruth smiled, but then her facial expression changed suddenly. She folded her arms over her belly. "I feel sick," she muttered.

That was when I actually heard Margaret's tummy growl beside me. In fact, it was more of a roar. "Oh no!" she cried. "Me too!"

I looked from Margaret's face to Ruth's and back again. They were contorted in pain. *What is happening?* I wondered, hoping I wouldn't be next.

"The cake!" shouted Margaret, pointing at it like it was a hand grenade with the pin pulled out. Then she jumped up and ran towards the bathroom, shouting at Jessica to hurry up.

"There's another bathroom upstairs," panted Ruth. "But I bags it!"

She darted off down the hallway, leaving me alone to ponder the closing credits of *I, Claudius* and my on-the-nose chocolate cake. Had I poisoned my new friends?

I sat on the couch for a while and horror started flooding through my veins. It didn't matter whether there was something wrong with the cake or not. I was going to get the blame.

The only thing to do was leave. I pulled out my phone and called Mum.

"Can you come and pick me up?" I pleaded.

"What's going on? I thought you were going to be there all afternoon."

"I thought I was too, but everyone got sick."

"Are you okay?"

"I think so. Can you come and get me?"

"Dad and I are having lunch at the yacht club with the Caves." Mr. Cave was my Dad's boss. "I can't leave now, Ally. We're just about to sit down to lunch. Can you wait a couple of hours?"

"Mum, *please* …" I felt bad putting pressure on her, but I had to get out of this place. "I don't want to stay. I hardly know these people."

"Oh, Ally," Mum said. "I can't come now, but I'll see if I can arrange for someone else to swing by."

"Thank you!"

"And I meant to ask you," Mum said, lowering her voice to a whisper. "This is a bit embarrassing, but did you take some laxatives out of my handbag?"

"What? No way."

"It's just that I bought a packet of a hundred Choc Laxettes yesterday. I'd put them in a ziplock bag in my purse, and when I checked just now, I noticed that about half of them are gone."

I gulped, my stomach sinking. "Choc Laxettes?"

"Yeah. They're laxatives. They make you need to go to the bathroom."

"I *know*, Mum!"

"Do you know where they are?"

My eyes shot to the half-eaten chocolate cake. "No."
I hoped I sounded convincing.

"All right, then. Perhaps they just fell out of the bag.
Now, sit tight and I'll arrange for someone to come and
get you."

I had only been waiting for a few minutes at the family
room window when I saw Gina Fini's 4WD pull into
the driveway. I was so relieved to see her I could have
cried. I didn't even shout a good-bye to the others, I just
escaped through the front door, feeling mortified.

I opened the passenger-side door and dived in.
"Thanks, Gina!" I gushed.

"It's no problem. I was already in the neighborhood
to drop Cat off at a soccer game."

I couldn't help smiling a bemused smile. "Cat is at a
soccer game?"

"Yeah. Cherrywood High's playing Penscombe
Grammar."

"I just didn't know that Cat liked soccer," I said. And then I remembered who played soccer: Ollie. And then I remembered who was cooking sausages at the soccer game: James. I asked Gina if she could drop me off at the game.

Gina agreed and did a U-turn. She drove me straight to the soccer match. "You should catch pretty much all of it," Gina said, as she pulled into the parking lot next to the field. Cat mustn't have told Gina anything about our fight because when she let me out of the car she said, "Cat's going to call me when it's over. I can give you a ride home."

I thanked her again and then took off across the parking lot towards the field.

The first person I saw was James, hunched over a smoking barbecue. But I ran straight past him.

I kept jogging until I spotted Cat. All wrapped up in scarves, she was cheering her lungs out over by the far sideline. Seeing her, I felt ecstatic. Tears welled in my eyes. Trying to make new friends had been so catastrophic. And it had made me determined to sort out our problems.

I raced through the crowd and didn't stop until I was behind Cat. Then I put my hands over her eyes. "Guess who?"

She wheeled around to face me. She looked confused, then relieved, and then as happy as I felt. "Ally! What are you doing here?"

"It's a long story," I explained. "I've got a lot to tell you."

Cat smiled and put her arm around me. "I can't wait to hear all about it."

Ally BUYS *treats* FROM the *bakery*

Chapter Nine

"You're spoiled for choice, Ally," said Mum. "Chocolate éclairs, caramel éclairs, cream puffs, apple danishes, lemon bars, Florentines, cupcakes ..." She was practically drooling as she peered into the glass display cabinet at the bakery.

"No cupcakes," I said firmly. "I think I'll get some lemon bars. At least it will look like I might have made them."

"Oh, Ally," sighed Mum. "Relax. I'm sure it's not a competition."

That's what you think, I thought.

We ordered a whole tray of lemon bars. While the

bakery attendant was packing them into a paper box, the door burst open and a gust of wind blustered around the bakery. The door slammed, sending the bell attached to it into a frenzy of dinging.

Then came a voice. "Twenty loaves of bread, please."

Mum and I spun around at the same time. I think we both wanted to see who planned to eat so much bread.

It was a tall guy in a scruffy beanie and a knee-length raincoat like a farmer might wear. "Oh, hey, Ally," he said. He pulled off his beanie. "It's James. Remember?"

I smiled, finally recognizing him out of uniform. "Oh, yeah," I said. "Hi!"

He looked so cute, even though he had terrible hat hair. It was sticking straight up like the bristles of a toilet brush.

"Um …" I was lost for words, paralyzed by the awkwardness of the situation. Here I was, caught in the act of buying something I was going to pretend was homemade. Mum standing right next to me made it all the more cringeworthy – for me anyway.

James didn't seem to mind. "Hello, Mrs. Motbey,"

he said politely. "I'm James. I'm in Ally's Latin extension class."

A bakery assistant was stacking loaf upon loaf onto the counter. I wondered just how many sandwiches James was planning to bring to the *I, Claudius* marathon. James unfolded two huge canvas bags from his big coat pockets.

"Let me help you," offered Mum, grabbing several loaves. "This is certainly a lot of bread."

"It's not for me," said James, chuckling. "I'm working the sausage stand at the school soccer game today."

"So you're not coming to the *I, Claudius* marathon?" I asked sadly. I couldn't hide my disappointment.

"No. I'd already promised to do the barbecue. Are you going to the marathon?"

"Yeah." I pointed to the lemon bars being packed away. "I didn't want to turn up empty-handed."

We stood there nodding at each other while Mum put the last of the loaves into the bags. "So —" we both said at the same time.

Mum seemed to pick up on the vibe. "Ally," she said

with a glint in her eye, "I'm just going to pop next door. Meet me there when you're done."

"Bye, Mrs. Motbey," said James, with a charming smile.

"Nice to meet you," Mum replied.

When she was gone, James stepped closer. I could smell the mustiness of his raincoat.

"To be honest," said James in a low voice, as if the bakery assistants were eavesdropping, "I probably could have blown off the barbecue and gone to Ruth's today, but …" now he was leaning in really close "… this is a bit awkward, but Margaret has a bit of a crush on me."

"Really?" I feigned ignorance.

"Yeah." He looked a bit troubled. "We had a deep and meaningful yesterday afternoon on the way home from school. She told me that she's been, well, you know …" his face was turning red "… noticing me lately."

My blood ran cold, but I tried to keep my voice even. "She's really nice."

"Oh, yeah, I know … it's just that I don't feel the same. Even though she's a great girl and everything. I told her that and she took it pretty well. I think she understood where I was coming from." He flattened his hair nervously with his hand. "I just didn't think it was a good idea to spend the day in a dark room together. Know what I mean?"

"I know what you mean," I said, my heart leaping. I was so relieved that he'd already sorted things out with Margaret.

He reached into his coat pocket and pulled out his phone. "What are you doing after the *I, Claudius* marathon?" he asked, looking down at the screen of his phone.

I kept my voice light. "Mum's picking me up. I guess it'll be pretty late by then."

James nodded. Then he took a deep breath and, still looking at his phone, said, "Can I call you sometime?"

I broke into a massive smile. "Of course!"

He looked up at me, finally, and smiled back.

Still grinning, I gave him my number.

"I'm kind of relieved," he said, slipping his phone back into his pocket. "I mean, you didn't sit next to me in class yesterday –"

"I was too nervous!" I admitted.

"I thought you were mad at me for scaring you in the library …"

"Not at all! That was funny, actually."

For a moment our eyes locked. He leaned towards me and I knew he was going to kiss me.

My heart started thumping. I had an unwelcome flashback to my terrible first kiss with Tony, but I shook it off. Nothing was going to stop me from enjoying this: not the bakery assistants gawping from the counter, not the idea of my mother stealing sneaky glances through the front window – and certainly not the thought of Tony Rickson. He was *so* last year.

James reached out and cupped the back of my head with his hand.

I closed my eyes. My skin broke out in shivers.

He leaned down and pressed his lips to mine. It was quick, but mind-blowing.

When I opened my eyes again, he was bending over to pick up the bags of bread.

"Bye, Ally," he said as he pushed through the

bakery door.

I couldn't believe how things had worked out. My heart and brain were both racing. James liked me! James had kissed me. Margaret knew that nothing could happen with James. I did feel a bit sad for her, but she was so gutsy and cool that I was sure she'd be okay. I hoped we'd still be able to be friends … Slowly, I came back to earth. That was when I realized I was still standing in the middle of the bakery.

One of the assistants, who was still hovering behind the counter, said, "Just as well he left when he did." She tittered. "I thought I was going to have to put out a fire!"

I was so embarrassed, I grabbed the box of lemon bars and ran for the door.

"Whoa, slow down there!" brayed Mum as I rushed straight past her on the street. I spun around to a stop, feeling slightly dizzy.

"Are you okay, Ally?"

"Yeah, I'm fine," I said, feeling light as a feather.

"Well, you're certainly keen to get to your friend's

place," Mum said with a laugh.

I grinned, blushing slightly. "I want to make a good impression."

"Well, darling, I'm glad you've met some new people. It's all very well to have a special friend like Cat, but you do need other friends too. Taking that Latin extension class was a great idea."

I shrugged as I stood at the car door. "Cat and I aren't as close as we used to be," I confessed.

"Maybe that's not such a bad thing," Mum said, opening her door. "You shouldn't put all your eggs in one basket when it comes to friendship." She ducked into the driver's seat and I got in the other side of the car, wondering if Mum was right.

Before Mum started the car engine, she turned in her seat and looked at me. "And that boy, James – what a lovely young man. It's not often you meet a boy that age with such good manners."

I looked away, pretending to fiddle with my seat belt. James's name made my cheeks hot. Then I thought about the way Tony had been treating me since our kiss, and how different things were with James. "No, it's not," I agreed finally. "Good manners are important," I said, grinning at Mum.

Can't get enough of

Choose your own Ever After?

Choose your own Ever After

HOW TO *Get To Rio*

BY JULIE FISON

HOW TO *Get To Rio*

For months *Kitty MacLean* has been crushing on Rio Sanchez – who is probably the cutest guy in the world. But it looks like she might never get a chance to hang out with him.

Until ...

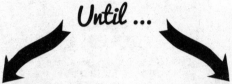

Kitty goes camping with her best friends like she promised them, and finds out Rio just happens to be staying not too far away. But should she meet up with him? Or is a grubby camping trip not the best time to meet up with your mega crush?

Kitty breaks her promise to go camping with her besties and goes to the beach with popular-girl Persephone instead. The offer is sweetened with a promise they'll definitely get to hang out with Rio. But should Kitty really ditch her friends to hang out with the cool girl? And will Rio even like Kitty?

In this pick-a-path story **YOU** get to make Kitty's decisions, and choose where her story goes. Follow your heart right to the end, or go back and *choose* all over again.

Choose *Your* *Own*
Ever After

A *Hot Cold* SUMMER

BY NOVA WEETMAN

A *Hot Cold* SUMMER

It's the last day of school and *Frankie Jones* is looking down the barrel of a long, hot, boring summer with only her guitar for company.

Until ...

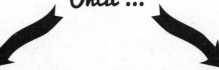

Frankie gets a surprise chance to go to London. She wants to go, but being in London will mean seeing gorgeous Jake again – the guy who broke her heart. Will things take up where they left off? Or will Frankie finally prove to herself that she's over him?

Frankie's dad invites her on a beach vacation. But when she discovers her dad's new girlfriend and her daughter, Ellie, will also be joining them, Frankie's disappointed. Will she get to spend any time with her dad at all? Or will she have to hang out with Ellie, her new best frenemy?

In this pick-a-path story **YOU** get to make Frankie's decisions, and choose where her story goes. Follow your heart right to the end, or go back and *choose* all over again.